Her Mourning Portrait

AND OTHER PARANORMAL ODDITIES

CEMETERY GATES
MEDIA

Her Mourning Portrait and Other Paranormal Oddities
Published by Cemetery Gates Media
Binghamton, NY

Copyright © 2018 by John Brhel and J. Sullivan

All rights reserved. Without limiting the rights under the copyright reserved above, no part of this publication may be reproduced, stored in, or introduced into a retrieval system, or transmitted in any form or by any means (electronic, mechanical, photocopying, recording, or otherwise) without prior written permission.

ISBN: 978-1983682797

For more information about this book and other Cemetery Gates Media publications, visit us at:

cemeterygatesmedia.com
facebook.com/cemeterygatesmedia
twitter.com/cemeterygatesm
instagram.com/cemeterygatesm

Cover design by Ben Baldwin

Contents

Introduction   5

Her Mourning Portrait   7

Side by Side   21

Lady of Cayuga Lake   29

The Lost Cache   47

The House on Pearl Ave.   57

With These Rings, I Thee Dread   75

Mr. Green's Passional   81

Her, He, and a Corpse Makes Three   91

Play it Again, Sam   107

Beyond a Blood Moon   127

Previews   131

Acknowledgments   155

4

Introduction

With this collection, we aim to present the difficulties of sustaining flesh-and-blood relationships through a novel lens: the weird and uncanny. Paranormal themes and plot elements help us explore interpersonal relationships in unique, often amusing, ways; but at their core, these tales are not about ghosts or strange premonitions—they're about flawed, everyday individuals navigating the complexities of dating, marriage, and loss. If anything, the strange situations that our characters encounter only parallel the seemingly arbitrary, uncertain nature of real-life love and companionship. And while you may not ever communicate with a dead lover or have a preternatural insight into a different time or place, you can likely relate to the tragedy, the euphoria, the *insanity* that the act of loving often entails.

The following stories are romances in the broadest sense. Each tale is built around a central character's quest for a more secure, fully actualized, and loving intimacy. However, most of the stories would not properly fit within the expectations of the already established paranormal romance subgenre.

With books like *Tales from Valleyview Cemetery* and *Corpse Cold: New American Folklore*, our goal was to entertain readers with spook stories featuring uncomfortable plot elements that approached real-life horrors; and in *Carol for a Haunted Man*, we portrayed a helpful, Dickensian apparition, and a mortal protagonist who was struggling to rebuild his personal and professional lives. While this collection is a mix of both thematic styles, we hope to satisfy both readers who've enjoyed our campfire oddities and those who've preferred our more literary moments.

John & Joe
February 2018

Her Mourning Portrait

A blank canvas sat on an easel in one corner of the artist's studio. The artist's tools—the paints, brushes, pencils, and turpentine—remained at ready for an artist's hand to put to use. However, this studio had, over time, become the daytime sick room for the artist's wife, and paints were no longer thinned in this space, and new canvas had not been stretched here in nearly a year.

Charlotte Kloone lay in a small bed across from wide French doors, which led out to a patio and well-manicured gardens. Her husband, Jackson, the painter, sat bedside, reading interesting pieces from the papers, often searching for his wife's reaction to the news. Her chlorosis and underlying disease left her skin pale, tinged green; she was a shell of the woman he had known for the twenty years since college.

At forty-two, Jackson had found success on the merits of his art alone. Charlotte, at forty, had found herself diminished, a victim of a multi-year, heart-rending descent from her personal and professional successes. Her fall had begun only months after the discovery of her first pregnancy. The tests revealed a dormant condition. The miscarriage became a certainty.

While Jackson sat beside her and read from papers, books, and magazines, commenting on the things which had been of interest to her in her previous life, she distracted herself from her present by reordering her memories and experiences in reverse, from the notable moments that led to their successes and freedoms back to the struggles of a high school art teacher and civil lawyer.

Charlotte would often study her husband's aging face while he read, remembering him as he was at twenty-two, imagining him as he would be at eighty-two. She watched him read and check on her, and would avert her still lively, green eyes—having been caught—to the pink orchid which stood potted on the nightstand next to the bed, a gift from Jackson.

"You're not interested in the news today?" Jackson smiled, having spied her staring at him blankly.

"Am I getting lighter, Jack?" replied Charlotte.

"Your skin tone, or your weight, Char?"

She laughed faintly. "Both, I guess."

Each morning he carried her from their second-floor bedroom down to her makeshift day bedroom in the art studio. They were months beyond trips outside in the wheelchair, weeks past sitting in the parlor watching TV together. The doctor now came to her.

Jackson placed two fingers beneath her wrapped torso and pretended to lift her. "You're light as a feather, stiff as a board." He then lifted her hand for inspection. "Your skin is a soft mint cream on a human-beige palette."

Charlotte smirked, then yelped when he licked the back of her hand and proclaimed her taste 'undefined.' "Speaking of palettes—why won't you paint something, already?"

Jackson hesitated. Everyone needs distractions, in even the most miserable of circumstances. "I, uh…what would I paint? I've painted everything." Neither could hold a straight face, but he cracked first, the edges of his lips curling.

"How about my orchid? It's lovely in the evening, with the way the light comes in from the doors," replied Charlotte.

"Okay." He nodded, but had to look away, due to the high albedo of her morning cheery self. "Let's get back to the president and the bombings, very serious matters." He knew how quickly she wilted in the early afternoon, and sometimes wished he could skip the morning altogether, because of how much he lost of her to post meridiem daylight.

Jackson had no intention of painting that night, or ever again, for that matter. But he found himself alone in his studio, contemplating a blank canvas, while his wife slept uneasily upstairs. He half-heartedly positioned the pink orchid near the easel, knowing he wasn't going to paint it. Instead, he flipped through an old photo book, images of vacations, day trips down the Hudson River by kayak, wedding party photos. His nostalgia sparked a creative fervor, energizing him. He painted a portrait of his wife as she had been years before, a picture of health and beauty—while simultaneously grieving the loss of her, as she was and as he had once dreamed she'd be.

When he brought her down to the studio the next morning, he hesitated with her in his arms in the stairwell, worried how she'd react to his night's work.

"Wait a minute, Jack." Her face had deflated on their march down the hall, from her usual morning show of optimism. "Maybe I'll stay upstairs with the nebulizer this morning."

Jackson didn't reply, but turned on the stair with her ninety-seven pound frame, moments later placing her back in bed with little fanfare.

"Please, don't put me in the ground just yet, Jack."

"I'm sorry. I had a small surprise for you downstairs."

She smiled faintly. "Tomorrow then?"

He nodded. "Should I call Dr. Shah?"

"Yes, I think so," replied Charlotte.

Jackson got her situated, then went down and made the phone call, which was now routine, and didn't have the air of an emergency that it once had. Charlotte wasn't well that morning, and it would certainly be an eventful day. Jackson would have to remember to cancel a visit from one of his old students that afternoon.

When he went to his studio to finish cleaning up his paints and work area, he found the orchid wilted and unrecoverable. He cursed himself for moving it, assuming that he had placed it too close to the French doors the night before, allowing the late-fall chill to denature the flowering plant. He thought it ironic that he had never intended to paint it for preservation and had valued it far more as a fixture of the room.

The portrait of his wife as a young woman brought him surprising satisfaction that morning. The detail he had put into her strawberry-blonde hair was photorealistic. It was as if it wasn't by his hand, and he could admire it as a work of some other master. He took time out of his busy morning to sit with the painting but was soon brought back to the present by Dr. Shah's visit.

The doctor didn't mince words after his quick analysis of Charlotte's deteriorating condition. "Mr. and Mrs. Kloone, at this point in the illness, I would recommend comprehensive, aggressive in-hospital treatment, or hospice care."

"I see no reason to go to the hospital," replied Charlotte, matter-of-factly. "We've had a plan for if the treatments failed."

Jackson didn't say much during the visit. The doctor and Charlotte negotiated the small things regarding the end of one's life. The hospice team would be contacting the Kloones within days, if not by the next morning.

When Dr. Shah left, Jackson went back down to his studio, without a word passed between him and his wife, and destroyed the room. He smashed the furniture against the walls and tossed all his painting tools. Paints splattered across the floor and rugs, though the portrait of his lady went untouched, and the wilted orchid in its pot went unharmed by the rampage.

Jackson didn't scream, or howl, but tore at his beard and receding hairline. He banged his head against the walls and floor, and cried silently. He welcomed his feelings of rage and grief as healthy expressions of his grief, as natural as the feeling of satisfaction and joy one gets from having loved someone, or having created something of value.

10

Upstairs, Charlotte was entirely aware of what was transpiring below, and grieved for her husband, while experiencing the same emotions as him. She thought of his future after her; the process of him aging and her remaining ageless in death, an unchanging remembrance—whether the memory of her at age forty and ill, or at twenty and the picture of youthful exuberance.

Days of anguish passed for the couple, before a hospice nurse arrived to assist in the final weeks of Charlotte's life. However, Charlotte felt well enough that morning for a trip through the back garden in her wheelchair, an activity that the Kloones had long given up on. It was a cold morning, and the nurse objected, but they bundled Charlotte in a heavy winter coat and blanket, and Jackson pushed her across his wrecked studio, through the French doors and out onto the stone patio.

"I would say I like your painting, but it wouldn't be very modest of me," said Charlotte, in a near whisper.

Jackson didn't respond immediately, but wheeled her around the back patio and along the walkway that led down a slight embankment to their trellised garden. Withered brown grapevines crisscrossed the white patchwork of the trellises.

"It came to me in a fit of inspiration, as you can probably tell from the state of things," replied Jackson, chuckling.

They laughed together for the first time in days. "Yes, I'm just glad you didn't toss our orchid too."

Charlotte didn't have to ask, or even comment, on why he had destroyed his workspace.

"I feel almost like months have been rewound. Not like I'm getting worse at all," said Charlotte, hazily. "I know it might be fleeting, and Dr. Shah is the expert, but I feel very much alive this morning."

"Living and breathing," stated Jackson. "You look kissable this morning."

"I don't know. We should consult the good doctor first, see if 'kissable' is a diagnosable condition."

Jackson bent down to her, nose to nose, and she kissed him on the mouth. It was the first proper kiss they had shared in weeks, and he was self-conscious of his chapped lips.

"Don't overthink it, Jack. Just kiss me."

And it wasn't only that morning that Charlotte felt time rewind. During those winter months, she regained her color and her health. She could again sit with her husband and enjoy life, and then walk, and then leave the house. Dr. Shah declared her in full remission the following March.

Jackson reclaimed his studio, repairing the damage he had done. The sickbed was thrown out, but he left the painting and the wilted orchid in the room as they were, untouched, out of superstition. He went so far as to place a glass dome over the orchid and a plastic gate around the easel, which still held the painting of his wife in full health.

The Kloones went on to spend ten joyous years together, and Charlotte was the picture of health, returning to her work while her husband took on students at home. Their life was rich in experience and they reinvested in each other; and Charlotte hadn't a grey hair or worry in those ten years.

Another ten years passed, and the pair approached sixty as companions, embracing the intimate friendship that gradually replaced the passion they had in their first thirty years together. Jackson was now bald, with some grey remaining around his ears, and had lost some of his posture, gaining a slight, contented belly. Meanwhile, Charlotte remained as youthful as the picture he had painted. She hadn't aged a day beyond forty and felt a certain vibrancy that Jackson had aged out of.

Jackson had taken on the pains of the aged man. But his life's difficulty was more than his entrance into old age, more so watching the eyes of his striking, spry wife wander. Younger men noticed her at age sixty, just as they had when she was thirty and forty. He was fully aware of the reason that she had ceased responding to him physically, why her passion for him had faded. She was the picture of a woman-in-full, something to behold, while he was a faded, weary facsimile of his former self.

Jackson assumed she was seeing someone when she began going out at night to shop or meet with friends. The late-night rendezvous is never something routine. The conversations in other rooms, messages sent back and forth at all hours—a new romance can never properly disguise itself or be contained to merely quiet hours.

But what hurt him the most was discovering that her dalliances were with one of his own students—28-year-old man that he considered one of his closest friends; a man he had invited into his home and studio, had fed at his dinner table. It was too much for Jackson. To let it go on flew in the face of everything they had promised each other over the decades after they had been given a second chance together.

"It's Paul, right?"

"What's that, Jack?"

Charlotte had just come home, well after midnight.

"My student. You're sleeping with him," stated Jackson.

Charlotte was wide-eyed, a deer caught. "It's that obvious?"

"Yes. And I really can't believe, after all we've been through, you can be this nonchalant about it."

"Please, Jack, there's nothing easy about it. We aren't the same people. I love you, but not the way I did when we were thirty."

Charlotte tried to walk off, but he grabbed her by the arm. "We grew together, and you really just want to throw it all away? For what? *Sex?*"

She yanked her arm away. "I love you and I'm your wife, but I don't wake up every morning like you do, aching and miserable. If *you* represent what one's supposed to feel, and act like at sixty, then I don't want to feel or act sixty."

Charlotte left the house before her husband could properly have it out with her. Jackson stormed into his studio and again destroyed everything in the room—everything except the decades-old painting on the easel, which he held sacred. He stopped himself before he stomped a hole through his wife's image. However, during his rampage he knocked the wilted orchid and its glass case to the ground, shattering the covering and partially crushing the long-dead, mummified flower inside.

He didn't hear from Charlotte for days. He partially cleaned up his studio, setting the plastic gate back around the easel that held her painting and putting the damaged orchid back on the shelf sans covering. During his time alone, he did what he had always done when faced with life's difficulty—he painted.

Jackson recreated the orchid as he remembered it, from back when Charlotte was approaching death. He took solace in resurrecting the past in that room, drinking and reminiscing about forty years of loving another person wholeheartedly. And a strange thing occurred in that studio once Jackson passed out that night. He awoke late the next morning to the splendor of a living orchid where a husk had been just hours before.

That day, he left his studio only to tend to his most basic needs. He sat and contemplated the vibrant orchid which sat on his shelf, and the one sitting on his easel. What was the mechanic? Had he recreated reality with his thoughts alone, or was it through the act of painting? It didn't anger him then, when he caught the last rays of day hitting the painting of his wife in the corner of the room, realizing then the gift that he had bestowed upon his beloved twenty years prior.

Jackson went to work that night, painting himself as he was at forty. He pored over pictures, studied himself in the mirror, and tried to smooth out the wrinkles and creases in his skin, to recreate himself as he was—his wife's equal. His self-portrait was an exhausting night's work, and when he fell asleep, he felt as content as he had when they were forty-five and fifty and still passionately dedicated to loving each other.

Jackson was awakened that next morning by a phone call from his wife. He slowly approached the hallway mirror as he paced, and they talked, and he nearly dropped the phone when he saw himself—the portrait of age sixty, wrinkles and all, another day older. He half-heartedly listened to Charlotte's repentant pleas and didn't care much when she reiterated her passionless love for him. He couldn't take her promises to him seriously—that she could still be faithful, or even the possibility that they could one day return to the life they'd built together. But he did agree to meet with her the following day.

Jackson knew he still had a choice to make. He considered painting his wife as an old woman or even destroying the original painting in the hours leading up to their meeting. He drank whiskey and readied a new canvas that evening, facing the ikon of his wife's portrait, preparing to begin his task.

But the next morning, the morning of their meeting, he awoke to the sight of the blank canvas, and the same unmarred portrait of his youthful Charlotte. He couldn't bear the thought of what might've happened had he destroyed the painting.

Jackson arrived late for the meetup with his wife. He didn't hold back. He told her what he had discovered of the paintings, his power. He wanted to show her the orchid as proof.

"Jack, you're hungover and talking like a complete idiot."

He wondered if she had been staying with his student that week. "Char, I'm just asking for your permission to destroy the painting. I've been going over it for days. I don't think I can just paint you old." Jackson was rambling. "I think maybe things will be set right then, and we can have a third chance with each other."

"Actually, maybe you're still drunk, Jack," stated Charlotte. "I've noticed your drinking problem the last couple years, but it seemed harmless enough—the excesses of the artistic impulse. But now you're coming off as genuinely crazy, delusional, and I'm reconsidering..."

Charlotte lit a cigarette, something he hadn't seen her do since before she had gotten sick all those years ago.

"You're smoking now? Is that something you and Paul have in common?"

She ignored his question, but freely admitted her connection to his ex-student.

"Just come see the orchid, Charlotte."

She sighed. "I'm not coming home, Jack."

"You said you'd love me forever."

"I will love you forever. We'll always be together in spirit—at twenty, thirty, forty, and so on. Love itself is everlasting, but the passion that accompanies love isn't meant to be this undying fervor, Jackson."

"Well, it is for me, Char. I love you as immeasurably as I did at twenty or thirty or last week—as I do now." Jackson was now shaking. "And I can't believe you're saying these things to me. I can't imagine living to be sixty and never having truly loved someone else. Because *real* love is precisely that thing that is unfading, and always imbued with passion, regardless of the age of it."

Jackson returned home, alone, and began working on a new painting. He worked into the night, feverishly, soberly, after the confrontation with his wife. When he finished his new painting, he found the old mattress and the frame to the sickbed in the attic, and set the bed up in the studio, where he fell asleep.

The following evening Charlotte returned home. She felt terrible about how she had spoken to Jackson the day before. She wanted to have some sort of relationship with him, even if it wasn't exactly what either of them desired.

16

It felt strange to her, knocking on her own front door. Jackson didn't answer, so she walked in. His car was in the driveway, so she only had to find him. She didn't bother checking the upstairs bedroom but went right to his studio, figuring he'd be slumped over in a chair, among his works. Memories came to her as she walked the long hallway toward his room, and she shivered when she caught a reflection of herself in a mirror. It all felt unnatural, as if she had been absent for years and was only now returning.

When she opened the door to the studio, she saw her painting first, the same as it has always been, but was taken aback at the sight of her husband's newest creation. It was a self-portrait, but not of Jackson at sixty, or even of him much younger, to match her painting. No, Jackson had painted himself thirty years *older*.

When she stepped into the room and saw him lying in her old sickbed, aged an additional thirty years and seemingly near death, she shrieked and crumpled next to him in shock. She studied his new, intense wrinkles, ran her hands over his weathered, drooping face. Jackson made no response. He merely wheezed and sputtered as his youthful wife studied him.

Charlotte then spotted the living orchid on the nightstand. It was suddenly as if she had been transported back decades, but now she was in the position of her husband, mourning her dying spouse.

"You painted the orchid? It's alive, Jack. Oh my god, Jack. It's alive!" She placed her head to his chest and listened to his heart faintly beating, his now-shallow breathing. She heard his final heartbeats and wept, pleading with him to remain with her.

Jackson passed away in her arms. She screamed, tearing at her hair and clothes, slapping her face and beating her chest over how flippantly she had treated him and her love for him. She looked at the three paintings in the room and cursed that he had given her the gift of extended youth.

17

Charlotte sprung from her husband's deathbed and grabbed his and her paintings, pushing open the French doors and tossing both portraits onto the patio. She ran to the shed where they kept the mower and gardening tools and grabbed the gas can, returning to the patio and dousing the paintings. She lit them and watched them burn, tears streaming down her cheeks. When she was sure they were nothing but ash, she returned to her husband, lying by his side, eventually falling asleep.

Charlotte awoke the next morning to a glint of light in her eye, reflecting off a broken shard of glass in the corner of the room. A ray of sunlight hit the orchid painting in another corner and a flood of despair came over her, as she realized where she was and what had happened. She turned to her dead husband and embraced him, her head on his still chest.

She lay there for some time, not ready to accept that Jackson had made his descent into nothingness—that his body was some separate vessel from the man whom she had spent countless intimate decades with. She was resigned to lay in that position for hours, for days—but then was startled from her malaise by the slightest movement of his chest against her cheek. Charlotte quickly sat up, and madly slapped at his cheeks and chest, at first disbelieving her senses. "Jackson! Jackson!" She sobbed when he opened his fearful, glazed-over eyes, watching as he searched for something to anchor his conscious mind to.

He smiled at her when the Promethean spark finally took hold within him. "It's nice to see you, too."

The couple spent hours in bed, investigating each other and talking over what had occurred. They slowly got out of bed, physically and emotionally drained; they supported each other and walked out into the hall. Together they looked into the mirror, really seeing each other for the first time in decades. They looked their true ages, sixtysomething. Charlotte had gray hair and crow's feet for the first time in her life. She felt the soft pouches beneath her eyes and her drooping ear lobes, and laughed at the new position of her breasts. Jackson, having shed thirty years from the previous evening, again felt his natural, aged self.

That morning they bathed together and had breakfast, unable to take their eyes off one another, staring intently, as if they hadn't seen each other for a lifetime.

20

Side by Side

Anna Ward lay sick in bed, as she had for months, contemplating the marriages that had defined so much of her life. With little to do other than watch television or read, her thoughts often turned to the past, when she felt *alive*, and could still get out of bed on her own. In her 91 years, she had been the object of affection for not one, but two upstanding gentlemen, for which she was beyond grateful. But when her health dramatically declined, her marital history became a source of intense anxiety for Anna. She was unprepared to tackle the subject of her burial when her husband, Michael, finally brought it up.

"Anna, I know about the plot Edward bought for you, but I think you should reconsider," said Michael.

"He was my first love, Michael. I feel like I owe it to him. He died believing that I would rest beside him. I made a promise. It seems wrong to deny him that."

Michael took a seat at the end of the bed. "You can't expect someone to stay single their whole life and to stick to some silly promise from decades ago. You're not a bad person for leaving that plot next to him empty. You're a woman who's been happily married for a very long time."

Anna thought back to the final days of Edward's life, the pancreatic cancer that had eaten away at him so quickly. Even after all the years that had passed since, she could picture his sickly-yet-still-handsome face, could smell the acrid aromas of that hospital room. To betray his trust, decades later, somehow felt wrong. But at the same time, it felt equally wrong to deny Michael, a man who had been her rock for so many years, of this one last request. "It's difficult, Michael. I don't want to hurt you, and I don't want to break my promise either."

"Not to be crass, but he won't know one way or another. And think about where you'll be buried. The plot I'm looking at is up on the hill, on the newer side of the cemetery. It's well-manicured, and there are beautiful maple trees all around. Edward's grave is along that old, rusted fence with the overgrown bushes. I'd like to be near you, in a nice spot."

"Oh, Michael," said Anna, softly. "Does it matter where I am? I'll be dead. So will you." She managed a small, pleading smile.

"Even in death, I'd prefer to be by your side."

Anna sighed. "That's sweet, honey. I really mean it. I just don't feel like talking about it right now. I need some rest." She closed her eyes and began to drift off.

"I don't mean to cause you any anxiety. Sleep well, my love." Michael kissed her lightly on the forehead and left the room, hoping she would choose him in the end.

When Anna died just three weeks later, Michael was forced to handle the funeral and burial arrangements amid severe grief and depression. She had never expressed with any certainty where she wanted to be buried—neither written nor spoken—so Michael did what he felt right and requested that she be buried in a new plot, a companion plot, next to his. The tombstone bore their names: Anna Ward (1926 - 2017) and Michael Ward (1932 -).

Anna's service was small, attended by her and Edward's children and the few remaining family members in the Binghampton area. Michael gave a heartfelt eulogy, speaking with great affection for his deceased wife about how they met working at the *Lestershire Bulletin*, her fondness for Lawrence Welk, their unforgettable trip to the Poconos in the early 80s. "39 years," he said. "And I'd have happily done 39 more."

As he gave his eulogy, and then saw his fellow mourners off, Michael failed to notice the man who had been watching

22

from a nearby maple grove—a man who had walked from his grave in Section 44 to get a glimpse of the ceremony. An enraged corpse by the name of Edward Barker—Anna's first husband.

Edward had sensed Anna's death the moment it occurred—a unique bond forged by decades of love—and had been eagerly anticipating her arrival. After all those years, she would finally be reunited with him. The date of their reunion would be etched on their shared tombstone, memorializing their new beginning. But it hadn't happened, and he was livid, to say the least, as he watched Anna's coffin being lowered into the ground in the newer section of the cemetery, up on the hill with the larger monuments.

Edward called out to Michael, who now stood alone, weeping, next to Anna's open grave. "Hey, Champ! What the *hell* do you think you're doing with my girl?!"

Michael turned to see Edward approaching him, a veritable husk of a man, in a nice, however dated, three-piece suit. He gasped at the sight of the corpse's uneven decay. The embalming process had not been kind, preserving one arm and parts of Edward's face and neck, grotesquely preventing nature from taking its course. Michael took a step back, and nearly tumbled into his wife's grave, but caught and steadied himself at the last second, using one of the nearby tent poles.

"Yeah, I'm talking to you," said Edward, stepping closer, his bones audibly cracking beneath his now-oversized suit. "You *jackass*. She's supposed to be buried next to *me*, down there." He pointed to the old section of the cemetery, in which he had spent four lonely decades.

"Who *are* you?" asked Michael, trembling, but somehow adjusting to the man's everyday demeanor.

"*What?* You've never seen a picture of me? I'm Ed Barker, Anna's husband."

Michael slowly began to realize just who he was talking to. He had, after all, walked past the dead man's portrait in the hallway every morning and every evening for as long as he had been with Anna. "Hate to break it to you, Ed, but you look worse off than some of the guys from my platoon who didn't make it home from Korea. Besides, Anna only has one husband. *I'm her husband.*"

"I was hers first, pal," said Edward. "And she made a promise to me. She's—"

"I know all about the plot," said Michael, his anger quickly eclipsing his initial fright. Anna was *his* lawful wife. "You've been dead for—what—42 years? She was with me longer than she was with you. You weren't there for her when she really needed somebody, to help her get over her grief, to care for her while she suffered from her sickness. *You* didn't have to watch her wither away into nothing."

The walking, talking corpse pointed a finger at Michael. "Listen here, son. I was knee-deep in blood and guts on the beaches of Normandy before your sack dropped. Anna and I had four kids and a good life together for over thirty years. You can either help me move her casket to its rightful resting place—to the plot which she and I purchased in 1966—or you can get in your car and screw off, and leave me and my wife to our eternal business."

Ed then stumbled past Michael to Anna's grave, knelt, and attempted to raise the casket, which was still cradled in the lowering device.

"You decrepit son of a bitch..." Michael took a few measured steps toward Ed and pushed him away from the open hole and onto the grass.

Ed groaned as he lay on his back and gathered what was left of his senses. His bad arm was now bent at an unnatural angle. "Ah, hell, son," he said, as he slowly managed to get himself upright. "If you wanted to tussle, you could have just said so." The corpse then smiled broadly at Michael, revealing recessed gums and eerily long teeth.

"Oh, I don't wanna just tussle, Ed. I'm gonna knock your mummy block clean off," stated Michael, stepping in to face his nemesis. "And quit calling me 'son.' I'm older than you by thirty-odd years now."

"I'm gonna bury you in this grave, *son.*"

"You think you're gonna put a hurt on me with that worm-ridden body of yours? Do your damnedest." Michael laughed. "I know that no matter what, when I die, *I'll* be the one buried next to Anna, and you'll be alone in your dingy hole."

With what little energy his rotting body could muster, Ed tackled Michael. But Michael fought back against the corpse, grabbing him by his withered frame and snapping his weak arm back, while Ed dug his skeletal fingers into the other man's skin.

Michael eventually managed to twist and rip Ed's arm completely out of the socket, and was holding it in triumph when Ed kicked one of Michael's weary legs out from under him. Losing his balance, Michael fell backward, and down into Anna's grave, his head smacking against the solid cedar casket.

Ed looked down at Michael's still body, which was draped across the casket. He waited for Michael to come to, and watched blood trickle from the man's head onto the flowers set atop the coffin lid.

"This is a real mess you've gotten yourself into, Ed…," Ed mumbled to himself as he paced about the burial site, trying to collect his thoughts. It would be near impossible removing both Michael's lifeless body *and* the casket with just one arm.

"*Edward*, what have you done?!"

Ed spun around to see Anna, her head and shoulders sticking out of the hole. It was his first glimpse of her in over 40 years, and had he any breath to give, she would've taken it away. The love of his life, and then some.

"*Anna*! Oh, I've waited so long!" Ed stumbled over to her grave, his remaining arm at ready for her embrace—but she raised her bloodless arms in defiance.

"You don't touch me. What have you done to my husband?!" She lowered her arms and looked down at her injured spouse. "Oh, Eddie… It wasn't his time to go."

"Your *husband?* We promised each other we'd be together for eternity. I can still hear it: 'Ed, I'll never love another man like you.' Didn't you mean it? I've waited for you for so long, Anna. You knew I'd be waiting for you. Why didn't you tell Michael you were to be buried next to me?"

"Ed, it's not that simple. I didn't know it was possible, but I loved Michael as much as I loved you. I didn't know there was so much room in a person's heart. But I never stopped loving you. It's all a big misunderstanding. My sickness came on so quickly, I never got a chance to decide between the two of you..." Anna trailed off as she dipped back into the hole.

Ed stumbled over to look down into the grave. He watched his wife cradle her second husband's head in her hands. She cried without shedding tears. "Gosh, I'm sorry, Anna. He ripped my wonky arm off and all—I didn't mean for him to fall into your grave like that."

Anna sniffed away her phantom tears. "Eddie, help me get him out. He doesn't belong in here like this."

The pair tried and failed, then readjusted and tried again, and after some time, they managed to maneuver Michael out of the grave and onto the cleanly cut lawn.

"I think he's still breathing," stated Ed, as he paced in front of the burial site.

Anna didn't look up from her second husband and studied his face for any sign of life as he lay unconscious. "Ed, it's probably best if you go back down the hill now."

Ed ached at the thought of it. *After all those years.* She had made her final decision, and he knew he must accept that she would lay beside Michael, and not him, until the end of days.

But as he began the long, lonely walk back to his grave, she called out to him. "Eddie, wait a minute, hon."

When Ed turned back, he saw her standing there in all her glory, in her prim, blue burial gown, beckoning for him to return. He swore she hadn't aged much, if at all, since he'd last seen her at Memorial Hospital, minutes before he, himself, had passed on.

Ed couldn't help but smile, walking back toward her. "You always were a looker, Anna. Even in death."

She didn't respond, but embraced him, and kissed him with the pent-up passion of decades. They stared into each other's dead eyes for a few silent moments, searching for lost time, before Anna spoke: "Eddie, you've got to go back to your grave and I've got to go back to mine. It's just how it has to be. We'll have some time together on the other side. I know we'll have some time if we make it—just you and me. Michael's younger, and healthy as can be. He won't complicate the matter for at least another decade, or so."

"Okay, Anna." Ed squeezed his wife's hand as they once again parted, then began his journey back to his final resting place.

Michael came to, unaware of the fact that his deceased wife had left her casket to confront Ed. But Michael sure was sore, and never seriously considered that he might have only imagined his fight with Ed; his black eye and bruised face certainly attested to the reality of the conflict. And he didn't quite know what to say when the caretaker returned to finish his wife's burial, and found him still sitting in the grass, his hair and suit dirty and disheveled.

It took some time and effort, but eleven years later, when Michael too passed on, he was interred beside his one true love—as was Edward. Michael had considered the quandary for quite a while before he had acted. Anna had loved her first husband as much as she had loved and cherished him—and he knew in his heart that she had never given him explicit permission regarding the change in her original burial plans. So, he made things right.

If you ever happen to be wandering through Valleyview Cemetery in Lestershire, you might notice two companion headstones sitting awfully close together. One marks the graves of Edward and Anna Barker, while the second records the burials of Michael and Anna Ward. Michael had to pull some strings, as it was an extremely unorthodox proposition, and it sure was a pricey maneuver. But when all was said and done, Anna was reburied in her intended plot, next to Edward, and Michael was put to rest in an adjoining plot. First lay husband, next lay wife, and then second husband—resting together. Side by side by side.

Lady of Cayuga Lake

Brian and Joan Kramer weren't planning a romantic week together when they booked a cottage on Cayuga Lake. For Joan, the trip was an opportunity to visit the sites of historic Seneca Falls and bask in the beauty of wine country, while Brian just wanted to visit a few distilleries, stock up, and spend his vacation in a constant state of buzz. It suited both their interests, and nothing more. Though they never discussed it—they never discussed much of anything of substance—both Brian and Joan had come to accept that their marriage was in its death throes. They had been living like roommates for years, and both quietly considered this trip somewhat of a "last hurrah."

It was a gorgeous July afternoon when they made their way toward the lake, Brian at the wheel. Countless white cumuli and rich greenery greeted the couple as they traversed the sun-kissed roads of Seneca County. However, the beauty and tranquility of their surroundings had yet to rub off on the couple. During their drive they had done nothing but display all their worst interpersonal behaviors, fine-tuned over a 15-year relationship. The pettiness. The false naivete. Deliberate misinterpretation of innocuous statements.

The car flew down the long road that ran parallel to Cayuga, the crown jewel of the Finger Lakes. They passed vineyard after vineyard, produce farms, and a variety of roadside eateries as they bickered about one thing after another.

Eventually, they turned off the main road and came to a series of handsome lakefront properties. Brian pulled into the

29

gravel driveway of a grey, four-bedroom cottage, a relic of the early 20th century. They got out with their luggage and went around to the side of the cottage to take in the lake. A dock extended 20 feet into the calm, blue water; three Adirondack chairs sat at the edge as at so many other New York lakefront properties, approaching a postcard ideal. The nearest residence was a comfortable distance away. It was the perfect place for a romantic weekend, were your name not Brian or Joan Kramer.

"This reminds me of your uncle's place on Lake George," said Joan, breathing in deep, basking in the scenery.

"Yeah, it does," said Brian.

"We had a great time kayaking and hiking. It was a nice, huh?"

"Yeah, it was a fun trip—if you don't include the whole wake and funeral thing."

"Of course, your great-aunt..." said Joan, sighing. "But why haven't we been back up there since?"

"I guess because no one's died." Brian smiled wryly, then took Joan's bulky suitcase. The couple went onto the screened-in front porch; a rustic, carved sign above the door read 'Pine Notch.' Brian removed the key from the lockbox, and they went inside. It was like stepping into a period film. Everything, from the furniture to the light fixtures to the artwork, was pre-WWI, save for a few modern amenities. The cottage was somewhat shabby overall, but still offered a keen sense of history and a vintage charm that, no matter your age or generation, reminded you of childhoods at the lake.

Brian set down the bags and returned to the car to retrieve the groceries. He met Joan in the kitchen, where they unpacked from a mid-morning jaunt to Machale Farms & Distillery. Joan sighed as Brian set a fifth of whiskey on the counter.

"Is there a problem?" asked Brian, pausing, though well-aware of what the problem was.

"No," said Joan.

"You're still mad about going to the distillery?"

30

"Forget it."

"You'll have plenty of time to visit the wineries," said Brian, already exasperated from a morning of passive-aggressive banter. "How was I supposed to know the distillery didn't have wine? We're in *the Finger Lakes*. They sell local wines at the CVS. There are tastings at half of the ice cream stands."

Joan had crossed her arms and was now standing sentry at the kitchen door. "I wish you'd told me where we were going, before I got myself all excited." She was rightly upset. Brian had promised her that they would have wine and cider at Machale's. "You could've even dropped me off at Chloe's Chakra Berry for the afternoon. We passed it before the distillery. They were having a special 'yoga in the vineyard' event today and I had my workout clothes with me." Joan looked at Brian's lineup of whiskey bottles. "Besides, you know I can't drink that stuff. I'd get drunk instantly and probably pass out!"

Brian snickered. "Would that be such a bad thing? Maybe you'd have some fun for once."

Joan pretended to laugh and wagged her finger at him. "Oh, you mean like you? Turn on the ballgame and pass out on the couch, with my hand in a greasy bag of Doritos?" She smirked, then left the room.

"*Bitch*," muttered Brian, under his breath. He opened a bottle of Machale's Finest and poured himself four fingers, before heading outside. Dusk had fallen, and the sky had taken on a peculiar shade of purple. He walked onto the dock and laid back in an Adirondack chair, reveling in the tranquility of his surroundings and the numbing effect of the alcohol.

Joan looked out from the kitchen window at the silhouette of her husband against the darkening sky. She had seen the open bottle on the counter when she returned from the bathroom and wasn't the least bit surprised. Brian had come there with his own interests in mind, as had she. But that didn't make it any easier—the painful, gradual

31

dissolution of their relationship. Joan had considered the possibility that they might reconcile some of their differences over the trip, at least make an effort; even Brian had an inkling, she knew. But, so far, neither had made a single attempt at empathy, tenderness, or understanding regarding their partner's needs and desires.

Wishing to occupy her mind, hoping to rekindle a romance somewhere—even if only in her imagination—Joan perused a small, built-in bookshelf in the living room. The books were aged, not only in appearance, but content: *Jude the Obscure*, *The Picture of Dorian Gray*. She picked up a copy of *Middlemarch* by George Eliot, and leafed through it. Many of the pages were stuck together, and they were brittle, easily tearing when she tried to separate them. It would be a real chore to read. But Joan was in the mood for a long British drama, something with a similar flavor to her favorite TV show, *Downton Abbey*.

She was surprised when a yellowed, unmarked envelope fell from the book to the floor. Picking it up, she pulled out its faded contents. It was a letter, which she opened and read:

June 20, 1912
Dear William,

I hope this letter finds you well, as you have been in my thoughts since our last "brush" on Decoration Day. I have recently fallen ill, but it is a bearable sickness, I can assure you. My parents are, as of yet, unaware of our circumstances. When I return to the farm it's as if I've entered a portrait of the last century. But it's far from lifeless in Lodi. My brother and sisters are as meddlesome and rambunctious as ever!

Oh, William. I can't stop thinking of your handsome face, your smart eyes and charming mouth. That you have given yourself so fully to a woman of my meager background, it means the world to me. I promise to serve you, to be as faithful to you as you are to me, for as long as we both shall live, and ever after.

32

I'm sorry for the brevity of this letter, but I'm penning it at the post office while my father barters with the smith. Here's to our separation being as abbreviated! To be in your arms in Seneca Falls!

Yours Always,
Mary

Joan smiled to herself at the earnest correspondence, though she did feel slightly voyeuristic in reading the century-old letter. She had only gotten a brief glimpse into the life of Mary, but Joan felt the woman's passion, and longed for a similar expression of love in her own life. She looked out the picture window and down at her husband, who sat on the dock. They watched the last, breathtaking gasps of twilight together, unbeknownst to Brian.

As the dark fully consumed the region, Brian and Joan were pulled from their ruminations by a sudden flash of white light from out over the lake. Just beyond the dock there was a pooling of energy, which seemed to emerge from the water like some sort of hallowed fountain. Brian, two glasses in, rubbed his temporarily blinded eyes, considering whether he had purchased a bad bottle of whiskey. It was almost as if a small lighthouse sat out over the water, illuminating the shore and cottage in a narrow band of light.

The situation only became more surreal as the water began to bubble and churn beneath the dock itself. Suddenly, a young woman emerged from the light, suspended over the water. She didn't appear wet or sodden in any way. She wore a light blue dress, and her long skirt obscured whether her feet met the water itself. Brian shuddered in his chair.

Inside the cottage, Joan watched at the window, taking in the same fantastic scene. She couldn't see all that Brian's position afforded him—details of the woman's dress, the sorrowful look in her eyes—but the effect was no less startling. The apparition then beckoned toward the cottage, causing Joan to shrink back from the window. She was frightened for Brian, and nearly called out to him. But as

33

quickly as the lady-over-the-lake had appeared, she, and the bright spectral light that accompanied her, dissipated.

Brian sat stock-still, anchored to the chair. The lake was now quiet, illuminated only by the lights from the cottages and a sliver of moon. He remained on the dock for nearly an hour, considering what he had just experienced. Joan watched him for a while, figuring he had been asleep during the unearthly occurrence. She went to bed but made a point to not drift off until she knew he was safely inside.

Breakfast the next morning was painfully quiet, even for the Kramers. Though both Brian and Joan had come to the same conclusion, over restless, sleepless hours—that they had witnessed a ghost—neither was about to cop to the other about such a ludicrous notion. They discussed their plans for the day—Brian would visit a popular brewery and bookstore, while Joan would stop by the Wesleyan Chapel, then shop to her heart's content at the Waterloo Outlets.

When Joan returned home that afternoon, Brian was already back, standing at the big picture window in the living room, staring out at the lake. "Have a good time?" he asked, without breaking his meditation.

Joan didn't immediately respond. The way he stood there, transfixed—in practically the same spot where she had borne witness the night before—she was certain that he must have also seen the ghost. But she held back, not wanting to make a fool of herself. "Yes. The vineyard was even more picturesque than the website made it out to be," said Joan. She smiled, yet her eyes told a different story. "What about you?"

"I'm fine," said Brian. He handed her a brochure. "If you don't have any definite plans for tomorrow, we could try this boat tour. I know history's your thing, and I'd love to see some of the big lake houses. I figure it's something we both might enjoy. What do you say?"

34

"Sure," said Joan, without hesitation. For the first time in a while, they had agreed on an activity without breaking into an argument.

She looked over the brochure for the boat tour as Brian wandered out back to grill up some steaks. It talked of architecture, natural history—the various selling points that Brian had mentioned—but what caught her eye was the brief passage on local legends, and more specifically, the haunted locations and *ghosts* of Cayuga Lake.

They had set out, a forty-minute drive from their cottage, near a popular shopping district, and were curious to explore the lake. It was a dreary, overcast morning when the Kramers boarded the pontoon boat that would take them on a guided tour.

A sixtysomething native who called himself Cap'n Jesse led the tour from behind the steering console, offering wildly interesting anecdotes from his well-traveled life, along with pedestrian details about the lake and its history: how it hadn't completely frozen over since 1912, its status as the longest of the Finger Lakes, and "Did you know *Twilight Zone* Creator Rod Serling once owned a vacation home here?"

Joan and Brian's ears perked up when Cap'n Jesse discussed the Guns of the Seneca, phantom cannon fire often heard by boaters out on the lake. He rambled on about this and other nautical folklore for several minutes, while commenting on one grand lake house after another. Eventually, he launched into a topic that piqued both Brian's and Joan's interest.

"We're approaching one of the more notorious cottages on the lake," said the captain, as they rounded a peninsula. "If you're into ghost stories, anyway." Brian and Joan both gasped when they saw where he was taking them—right to the very place where they were staying!

"How many of you folks are familiar with the story of Mary Gold?" asked Jesse. A few of the older sightseers raised their hands. "Excellent! She's had a bit of a renaissance since

35

one of our local authors, Lisa Peele, published a book about her life. But for those of you who don't know—way back, Mary became a symbol for the Women's Rights Movement at Seneca Falls. She was a tannery girl and a suffragette, and when she disappeared, just about no one seemed to care that she stopped showing up for work, or that her friends and family had reported her missing. But women in town, her comrades, rallied and caused a real uproar to get the sheriff to search for her." Jesse paused to draw in his crowd. "Sadly, she's most famous for never having been found."

Jesse killed the motor near Pine Notch's dock, before continuing: "Mary came from a family of farmers—poor, yet respected in their community further down the lake. She left her small town to come to Seneca Falls to work, and eventually joined the Women's Movement. At the time, there was gossip about a well-to-do bachelor named William Zane visiting the tannery girl unchaperoned."

Joan thought about the love letter she had found the day before, addressed to William, from Mary. *So that's William!*

Jesse continued: "When Mary went missing in July 1912, the story goes that there were certain influential folks in town who didn't want her to be found. She was last seen leaving a meeting with some of her fellow suffragettes at the Wesleyan Chapel. They were the women who forced the hand of the sheriff and got a respectable search organized. There were rumors of foul play, but nothing ever came of it. Back then it was 'no body, no crime.' They didn't have any of the tech you see on your crime-scene shows these days.

"I've heard from folks who've stayed at 'Pine Notch' here, and they say they've seen her around the property at night. It really seems like Mary is looking for William here at his family's cottage; whether out of love, or vengeance—the jury's still out on that."

Brian and Joan stared at the spot just beyond the dock where they had seen the ghost, then at each other. *Was it Mary Gold?* they both thought, as Jesse continued with the boat tour. They continued to look to the cottage, pondering its sorrowful history, as the boat travelled down the lake.

Following the curious excursion, the Kramers spent the remainder of the day shopping and dining. The couple chatted enthusiastically about the tour and the legend of Mary Gold's ghost into the evening, before returning late to the cottage to get ready for bed. In the bedroom, with its old-fashioned four-post bed and musty scent, Brian and Joan couldn't help but talk about the history of the house, even more so now that they knew the sad fate of one of the souls connected to it.

"Are you weirded out being here now?" asked Brian, as he slipped into bed next to Joan, who was reading on her tablet.

"It's strange, but I'm not scared." Joan avoided looking Brian in the eye, afraid she might reveal herself to him. "Do you believe this place is haunted?"

"You should look them up," said Brian, awkwardly avoiding the question. "I'm curious."

Joan opened her browser and searched for Mary Gold. They were taken aback when a black-and-white photo of Ms. Gold appeared onscreen.

"Oh, my god," gasped Joan, dropping the tablet to her lap.

"Wh- what?!" asked Brian, equally shaken.

"Brian, I have something to tell you—"

"You saw it, didn't you?!" he said, too excited to let her finish. "The *ghost*?!"

Joan nodded, then explained how she had watched the phantom appear from her place beside the picture window. He then recounted how he was so frightened that he couldn't move.

"I thought I was crazy," said Joan.

"No. You're not crazy," said Brian. "But why didn't you say something, since you saw that I was out there?"

37

"I don't know." Joan hesitated. "I figured that maybe you were asleep, since you didn't move, and I didn't want you to make fun of me."

Brian felt a pang of guilt over her response. "But what does it mean? A *ghost*? I thought she went missing. Like she was kidnapped or something."

"Just wait a sec!" Joan jumped out of bed and ran downstairs, returning momentarily with a yellowed parchment. "I found this in an old book. I think it was one of her last letters to William." She had Brian read the letter.

"Wow! What do you think this means? Why is she still hanging around?"

"Your guess is as good as mine," said Joan.

"What's her unfinished business? Her missing *body*?" asked Brian.

"It's terrible. And just imagine her fiancé," said Joan.

Brian looked his wife in the eye. "I remember when we were engaged. If you were missing, I would've found you no matter what happened—or died trying."

"Oh, Brian. C'mon," Joan grinned. "Have you been drinking?"

"A little," he said, "But I mean it." He startled her by pulling her close to him. "I'm not sure what's going on with this Mary Gold business, but I'm happy we're here."

Joan smiled. "Me too."

The couple made love for the first time in ages.

Joan awoke in the middle of the night, Brian sound asleep next to her. She was not a sleepwalker and believed herself to be in total control of her body, but she felt a strange compulsion to leave the room, walk down the hallway, and take the stairs to the first floor. The house was dark and every step she took was accompanied by the creak of a floorboard. She felt vulnerable, navigating a strange house in the dead of night, but continued. *Would she see Mary Gold out on the lake again? Would Mary beckon to her?*

38

Joan was already downstairs before she became aware of how bulky and tight her outfit was. She had gone to bed wearing a light nightgown and now here she was, three in the morning, dressed in a prim, powder blue dress that ran down to her bare feet! She even had a corset on. Before she had time to process why she was decked out in some century-old fashion, she was struck and shoved to the floor by an unseen assailant.

A man, his voice deep and seething with malice, stated: "It's not happening. I'm going to make sure of that."

Joan cried out, clutching her stomach in pain. She searched the dark room, trying to make out her attacker. As her eyes adjusted, a tall, young man with slicked black hair appeared over her. He was dressed in brown slacks, with suspenders over a white dress shirt. She would have thought him handsome, dapper, had he not just assaulted her.

The man picked her up, and Joan thrashed desperately against him. But before she could come up with a plan to defend herself, the man had already placed a rag tight over her mouth. Joan panicked; she couldn't breathe. All she could process was the noxious, penetrating scent of the ether as she attempted to scream...

"No!" Joan woke from her nightmare, uncomfortably warm, and slick from perspiration.

"What?! *What?!*" said Brian, jerking up in bed. "Joanie, what's wrong?!"

Joan buried her face in his chest and whimpered. "Who was that? Why'd he want to hurt her?" She described the dream to Brian, who consoled her for over an hour before they both fell back to sleep. Though it was just a terrible dream, Joan feared her attacker as though he was flesh and bone. This was a home haunted after all, and she didn't know if the man in her nightmare would manifest, as the ghost of Mary Gold had shown herself capable of doing.

The following morning Joan decided to look further into the Mary Gold story. She quickly found a webpage for a book entitled *A Suffragette Lost: The Mysterious Disappearance of Mary Gold.* There was a synopsis of the book and information about William Zane. He was only a name to her until that point, but the webpage offered a photo of him, grainy but clear enough for her to make out his all-too-familiar features. She had seen him before. He was the man from her nightmare!

Joan called Brian to the bedroom.

"What is it?" he said, appearing with a pair of steaming cups of coffee.

"William Zane, Mary Gold's fiancé, was the man in my dream."

"Are you sure?"

"Yes, and what's weirder is I'd never even seen a photo of him until just now." Joan stared at the tablet screen, her whole body tensed from her anxiety.

"Are you sure you've never seen a picture of this guy? We are in his family's cottage, and you did find some of his belongings."

"I'm sure, Brian," she replied, with certainty. She continued her train of thought: "Do you think William had something to do with Mary's disappearance?"

"Who knows? People come up with all sorts of reasons to hurt each other. Couples grow distant, jealous..." Brian paused, unsure of how to continue his train of thought.

"We can ask her!" exclaimed Joan.

"Do *what* now?"

"Tonight. We'll take a boat out and ask her. Two simple questions: Did William harm you? Where is your body?" Joan was practically shaking with excitement over her plan.

"Joanie, you want us to go out on the water and try to raise the dead? Ask a ghost a couple of simple questions?"

"You saw her, Brian! I think she was trying to get our attention. She needs someone to hear her story."

Brian chuckled, quite curious himself over the prospect of communicating with the dead. "Alright. You win. I'll find us a small outboard motor for tonight. And I think I saw a

Ouija board in the games cabinet beside the TV." He handed her one of the steaming mugs.

Joan crinkled her nose at her husband, before slapping him playfully on the back. "Thanks, Brian. This means a lot to me."

The lake, which was so beautiful and bustling with activity during the day, felt unnaturally still that night as Brian and Joan boarded the small boat Brian had rented. The water was tar black, calmly menacing beneath the faintest of crescent moons.

Brian piloted the boat to the spot where they had seen the ghost. Joan had brought with her Mary's letter to William, hoping it might aid in conjuring her spirit. Together they called out Mary's name, asking her their pre-planned questions, including "What happened?" and "Tell us your story," though Brian felt quite foolish in doing so. A half hour passed and there was no sign of anything unnatural.

"Mary must be taking the night off," said Brian. His voice was hoarse from shouting.

"We've got to be patient," replied Joan. She stared out into the night and called out again: "Mary! *Mary Gold!*"

"Maybe I was drunk the other night, or just fell asleep on the dock and had a weird dream."

"I saw it too, Brian, and I certainly wasn't drunk or dreaming."

"I'm just saying…"

"And what about my dream about William? And the letter?"

"What are the chances we're going to be able to contact, or even communicate with, a ghost? I doubt she's going to appear just because some tourists want to have a chat."

"So what, then? Do you think Mary ran off with some other guy and lived happily ever after in Ohio, or something?"

"It's possible. They never found a body."

"Yeah, we're probably wasting our time," said Joan. "But you might be onto something, Brian. She probably wasn't murdered by her rich fiancé. Maybe Mary, a smart, working-class suffragette, couldn't put up with her boorish, drunkard man, and ran off with a guy who actually felt passionate about her and what she was about."

"Hey, what's with the personal attack? All I said was it's probably going to be difficult contacting and communicating with this ghost." Brian laughed to himself. "I came out here and humored you. And now that you haven't seen your lady in the lake, you're upset and want to take it out on me? Christ, Joan, I was starting to have a good time with you, but I guess I was misreading the situation."

"Dammit, Brian! Think about someone besides for yourself for once!"

He had no chance to respond, as the placid water beneath the boat began bubbling, and was soon lit up in an ethereal greenish hue.

"She's here!" said Joan, excited.

But her elation was cut short by the sudden rocking of the boat over the now-churning water. She and Brian tumbled about the craft, Brian nearly over the side, as the lake came to life around them. They desperately tried to keep their balance, clinging to anything they could get hold of, as cold water sprayed in, soaking them on what was already a chill summer night.

"And we're *outta* here!" said Brian, grabbing the outboard motor. He squeezed the primer bulb, pulled out the choke, did everything he could to start the engine, but it was no use.

"Christ, it's dead!" said Brian.

"It's dead?! Why would you say *it's dead*?!" shouted Joan as she steadied herself in the bow. "Honey, what's that? I think..."

"This really isn't the time to chastise me over my choice of expression. I'm trying to get this thing going!"

"Brian, the light...."

42

Brian stopped what he was doing when he saw what Joan was referring to. The couple sat, fixated, as a series of fluorescent orbs darted around the boat and skimmed the water. Joan screamed when Brian was suddenly jerked up from his seat by some unseen force and thrown into the lake.

She attempted to rescue her husband from the dark, choppy water, nearly falling in herself. Joan then felt movement behind her and, before she knew it, she was yanked back by her collar and tossed onto the bottom of the boat. Standing over her was William Zane! He wore a sweaty dress shirt with the sleeves rolled up, and in his hands he held a rope.

Joan punched and kicked at him, but she was in such a weak position that there was little force behind her blows. William, unmoved and unflinching, tied the rope around her waist, which itself was tied to an iron anchor.

"You couldn't just keep your damn mouth shut, Mary!" said William.

"My name's not Mary!"

With the same carelessness with which he had tossed her husband, the ghoul picked Joan up and threw her into the churning, frigid lake. She was able to tread water as she fought the rope tied around her waist, clawing at the heavy knots with which she had been secured. Joan watched as William picked up the anchor with ease and tossed it in after her.

She let herself drift beneath the choppy water, counting the seconds until the rope would go taut between her and the anchor. She fought to loosen the rope as the dark rushed in around her. Joan could make out a faint, white light coming from far below, as though welcoming her to her final resting place. Soon enough her eyes began to cloud from lack of air and her exertion, and she felt herself go limp, passing out...

Joan regained consciousness as she was tugged back to the surface. She was still drowning as she was dragged over the lake toward shore. When her rescuer laid her down in the

43

grass, she was face down, choking and coughing up water. She felt a comforting hand rubbing her back as she regained her wits.

"You're alright, Joanie," said a familiar, masculine voice, his own breathing labored.

Joan eventually turned herself over and saw her husband above her, his hair, t-shirt, and khaki shorts saturated. "Brian!"

They cried and embraced before their eyes were drawn back over the lake by an emerging white light. Mary Gold appeared out of a haze near their now-capsized boat; she was looking at them distinctly, with purpose. The apparition soon faded into the night.

"What can you tell us about Mary Gold?" Joan asked the woman sitting behind a heavy, aged mahogany desk. She and Brian were in a small basement office at the Seneca Falls Library, the morning after their episode on the water. They had arranged for a meeting with Lisa Peele, Seneca Falls Librarian and author of *A Suffragette Lost: The Mysterious Disappearance of Mary Gold*.

Ms. Peele was an attractive woman, with a few silver streaks in her light-blonde hair, only a couple years older than the Kramers. "Well, have you read my book?" asked Ms. Peele.

Brian and Joan looked at each other awkwardly, unsure of how to respond.

"*Ha!* Of *course* you haven't!" said Ms. Peele, smirking. "I'm kidding. There's not much about the disappearance that hasn't made it to the Internet, anyway."

"Yes, we're curious if there's anything tying William Zane to Mary's disappearance?" asked Brian.

The librarian eyed the couple for a few moments. They didn't seem like cranks to her. "The stuff about murder and foul play was always just rumors—people with vendettas against the Zane family," said Ms. Peele. "As you probably already know, Mary Gold pretty much just vanished. No one, not William Zane, nor anyone else, has ever been publicly accused of having anything to do with her disappearance. There was no body, no suicide note, nothing of the sort."

"You don't think he did it?" interjected Joan.

"What I believe is purely speculative. I cover it in the last chapter of my book—which is for sale in our local bookstores," said Ms. Peele, grinning at the couple. "William Zane and Mary Gold certainly had some sort of relationship outside of the tannery. But there's never been any evidence, nor any reasonable theory presented, as to why William would kill her."

"Ms. Peele," said Brian, struggling to get the words out, "we believe we know what happened to Mary Gold."

Ms. Peele snickered.

"No, I mean it," added Brian.

"Right. You're here for a week-long vacation, and in that time, you've solved a hundred-year-old mystery—one which I've devoted decades of my life to."

"I don't discount all your research, but just hear us out." Joan recounted all the strange things that had occurred to the Kramers: the sighting on the first night, her dream about William assaulting Mary, and, finally, their adventure from the previous night.

"Ma'am. I'm also the *town historian*. My job is to collect and preserve the history of Seneca Falls, not to engage in paranormal investigations." Ms. Peele's demeanor and tone had changed drastically. "This was an important event in our town's history and deserves the seriousness of scholarly research backed by artifacts, evidence. Now, I hope you enjoy the rest of your vacation, but I have work to do."

"If you won't listen to us," said Joan, pulling out the letter that Mary had written to William, "take it from Mary Gold herself."

The historian rolled her eyes but took the letter and began to read. Brian and Joan watched, anxiously, as her eyes scanned the paper, and Ms. Peele's expression soon changed from one of disgust to giddy surprise.

"My god, this looks awfully authentic," said Ms. Peele. "Where did you *find* this?"

"In a book on a shelf in the Zane Family cottage."

"Do you understand what this *means?*" asked Ms. Peele, quickly deducing by their blank expressions that they didn't. "'*Brush,*' '*bearable sickness,*' '*circumstances.*' Mary was *pregnant*! No wonder the Zanes worked so hard to undermine a search for the girl."

"Oh, my god!" exclaimed Joan. "He killed her because she was pregnant!"

Ms. Peele called in a favor to the chief of the Seneca Falls Fire Department and a team of rescue divers arrived at the Pine Notch cottage early that evening. With direction from the Kramers, it didn't take long for them to discover the mummified remains of Mary Gold. Her waxen corpse was still tied by a rotting rope to a small, corroded anchor below.

Brian and Joan sat at the end of the dock, long after the divers, reporters, and Ms. Peele had left. Sure, the couple had their differences, and quite a bit of baggage yet to work through—but as they sat there, arms linked, Brian and Joan realized that they had something worth trying to hold on to.

The Lost Cache

No hobby provided Eric as much satisfaction as geocaching. He had spent the entirety of his Saturday tracking down caches scattered across the Binghampton area, seeking out containers that diehard enthusiasts like himself had hidden in the woods, along riverbanks, and tucked away in abandoned buildings. The caches were usually stuffed with tchotchkes, maps to other secret places, fossils—small tokens, really. The thrill of the hunt, the payoff, was in locating the caches, not the items themselves. Eric had checked off hundreds of caches in southern and central upstate New York—his find count was enviable—and he was spending every weekend driving down to the Catskill Mountains, and into the Finger Lakes, to up his tally.

"Hill, check out what I scored today," said Eric, as he walked into the living room of his apartment, tracking dirt, rock and other residue from the Slide Mountain Wilderness Area onto the carpet. He smiled, holding up a small button pin bearing the phrase "Cold Hard Cache."

His wife, Hillary, slowly turned her attention from the TV. "That's great. You spent all day out, and all you have to show for it is that button?"

Eric sighed. "I spent all day in the fresh air, *experiencing* the natural world."

"Any other woman would think her husband was having an affair—gone so much, and distracted when he's home—but the sad thing is, I know it's not another woman taking up all your time. You're literally just walking around in the

47

woods every weekend." She couldn't help but laugh, however bitterly, at the observation.

"Don't do this..."

"Don't do *what*? You said you'd be home in time for us to go out to dinner. I was looking forward to spending time with my husband for once. I'm not even mad. I guess I've gotten used to it—and I think I'm finally over it."

"It took a little longer than I expected," said Eric, to which Hillary rolled her eyes. He attempted to diffuse the situation. "You can come with me anytime you want, you know that."

"It's fun to hike occasionally, but what about what I want to do for a change? We work all week and have the weekends to unwind, and I'd prefer that we spend some of that time doing things together. We could have gone somewhere today as a couple. That curiosity shop on Antique Row. There was a strawberry festival in Owego today. But all I asked for was dinner, and you couldn't even..."

"You act like we never do anything together. We just went to Ithaka. I thought we had a good time?"

"That was over a month ago. You've gone caching probably half a dozen times since!"

Eric paused. He had plans to go on a three-day outing to the Adirondacks with his buddies, a trip he had yet to discuss with Hillary, and wanted to be in her good graces before broaching the subject. "Okay. How about we spend next weekend together? Just you and me."

"Are you sure?" asked Hillary, her tone softened.

"Of course."

"Luke told me we should check out Sylvan Beach on Oneida Lake. He said it's really nice. He goes there all the time with his brothers and family." Luke was one of her new coworkers. Eric had heard all about him the past few months, as Hillary was quite the social butterfly at the office. Hillary went on, talking about what they could do up at the lake.

"Then Sylvan Beach it is," said Eric, gently, breathing a sigh of relief that his wife now seemed placated.

Eric and Hillary drove to Sylvan Beach the following Friday after work. They settled into their hotel room and then enjoyed a nice meal together. Hillary proposed that they spend some time on the beach the following morning, but Eric killed the mood, announcing that he had made other plans. While he was booking their hotel, he had visited a geocaching website and added a few locations in the Sylvan Beach area to his watchlist. He told Hillary, who sat across from him dumbfounded, that he wanted to spend some time looking for them, and that it would only take a couple hours, that she could read some of her magazines by the hotel pool. With a sigh, Hillary let him go.

But by the time Eric returned from his trip the next day, the sun was already setting, and Hillary scowled at him as he traipsed into the suite.

"What the hell, Eric?! I asked for one weekend. *One weekend!*"

Eric took off his dirt-dusted backpack and kicked off his shoes. "I know, I know. I lost track of time. I'm sorry. It was a more rugged trail than I'd anticipated. The websites aren't always reliable." He really did get lost in his thoughts when he was alone in the woods. Timetables became irrelevant while he dreamed into his surroundings, took in the vegetation, and communed with the chattering birds and small woodland creatures.

"I should have known better. I can't even get one weekend with you. Christ, you're obsessed with this stuff. Why can't you just do normal guy stuff, like work on the house or watch baseball once in a while? Luke spends his weekends refurbishing antique furniture. Why can't you do stuff like that—at home?

Eric snickered. "Well, good for Luke. Sounds like a real adventurous guy."

Hillary glowered. "What a romantic getaway... Just don't even bother tomorrow. Go ahead and 'cache' all you want. I'll just do my own thing, you do yours."

"No, it's fine. We'll make it work. Tomorrow," said Eric, knowing that he had already tracked down all the caches in the area anyway. He could afford a day with his wife.

Hillary ignored him and picked up a romance novel from the dresser. "I'm going out on the balcony to read."

The next morning the couple merely packed and left. Hillary was exasperated and had no interest in forcing herself or her husband into a few hours of 'quality time.' The pair drove home in silence and quickly returned to their separate routines once their trip had concluded.

A few evenings later, Eric got home from work to find Hillary sitting on the couch, texting, as usual. He was about to retreat to his office when she said: "Hey, I heard about a cache you might be interested in."

Eric stopped, surprised to hear his wife bring up the topic, let alone offer anything more than a tepid greeting. "What?"

"It's in a cemetery an hour or so north of here, up Route 12. It's supposedly archived, but Luke says the box is still there. I'm actually curious about it myself and can meet you up there after work on Thursday."

"Really?" Eric smiled. He had gone hunting in cemeteries before, and the thought of tracking down a cache that had been taken out of play fascinated him. And he certainly appreciated not being harangued about his pastime for once. "Where is it? Does he have the coordinates?"

Hillary nodded.

"Cool," said Eric. "Hey, I thought you said Luke isn't into stuff like this?"

"He's kind of a Renaissance man," said Hillary. "He actually grew up not far from the cemetery."

"Okay. Well, thanks, Hill. I know this really isn't your thing, so I appreciate it."

"It's nothing. I have my passions, you have yours."

50

Eric had that Thursday off. He would go up before Hillary and locate the cache, as Luke said it was supposed to be a real chore to find, then Hillary would meet up with him.

Eric was packing his bag when his phone buzzed. It was a text from Hillary: *Here are the coordinates. See you in a few hours.* He was thrilled that his wife had finally lightened up and showed some interest in his hobby. He wasn't sure what had prompted her sudden change of heart, but he was pleased nonetheless. For the first time in a while, he looked forward to spending time with his wife.

He entered the coordinates into the CacheHunter app on his phone and a small blue dot started to blink on-screen. He was surprised to see the map zoom in on Oxford, a small town about an hour north of Binghampton, and then on Beardsley Hollow Road.

That's weird. He was familiar with Oxford and with Beardsley, as well. He and Hillary had picnicked in the cemetery up there, years prior, after chasing a legend he had heard about. This was long before he had fallen in love with geocaching. They had laid out a blanket next to a vault, on top of which stood a woman in mourning. Eric could still see her face, so striking was the statue and so memorable was the day. The statue was said to cry real tears at sundown on certain days of the year.

Eric still found it surprising that Hillary had agreed to go. But she had been more adventurous then. They had only met a few weeks before, and were giddy in their budding relationship, talking life and family, sharing intimate details. It had been some time since they enjoyed a day like that together. They couldn't seem to find the time anymore.

Eric got in his Jeep, mounted his phone on the dash, and took Route 12 north. He felt content, tracking down a mysterious cache in a place that held great meaning for him and Hillary, pleased that his wife had initiated the excursion.

He was halfway to Oxford when the sky darkened and rain began to batter the vehicle. He slowed down and thought about Hillary, hoping she would be okay driving through the

51

inclement weather. He considered calling her, but decided to hold off, as she hated it when he used the phone while driving.

When he eventually neared Oxford, he turned off Route 12 and drove down a series of weather-beaten, seasonal roads.

"Dammit! Are you *kidding* me?" said Eric. He hit the brakes as he rounded a sharp corner and the Jeep skidded to a stop in front of a metal gate. The road he knew that led past the cemetery itself was now closed, confounding him. He was still a few miles from the cache and hadn't anticipated having to walk so much of the way there, especially through the rain. It was, after all, an archived cache, and there was no guarantee that the journey would be easy. He grabbed his backpack and got out the car. It was mid-June, but the air was chilly due to the storm. He shivered as a brisk wind passed through the trees and lifted the back of his t-shirt.

He texted Hillary to find out how far behind she was, and to warn her of the unanticipated hike. He waited a few minutes, but received no response, and figured that his wife was still a distance behind. Phone service was spotty anyway. Eric decided to go forward without hearing from her, assuming they'd meet back at the gate regardless. Besides, he was still excited about finding the cache, despite the roadblocks. His love for the hunt pushed him on.

Eric was past the gate and into the woods when he noticed a fresh set of tire tracks in the mud; someone had been there recently. The road wasn't marked 'private.' Another cacher, perhaps? He shielded his phone from the rain and reopened CacheHunter. The app indicated that he could save some time if he left the road and walked a mile to the northeast. He stepped into the wet woods and pushed through underbrush and tall grass.

As he ventured further into the woods, Eric felt a type of anxiety that he had never experienced on any hunt prior. Maybe it was the weather. Maybe it was the mysterious cache. Maybe he wasn't doing enough to mend his fractured relationship with Hillary. Whatever it was, this was no cathartic jaunt through the natural world.

He walked among blackened, decaying pines, through some of the ugliest, burnt forested areas he had ever traversed. Several times he slipped over wet leaves or rocks and fell to the ground, cursing. His groans and complaints passed through the forest without response, and he became acutely aware of how alone he was.

After the dreary drive north and his slow progression through the forest, more time had passed than he would have liked, and Eric began to truly worry when dusk approached. He put on his headlamp and continued. He was shivering by the time he reached the crumbled wall that represented the boundary of the cemetery. The place was nothing like he remembered. The tombstones seemed more deteriorated, the ground uneven and rocky. It had been seven years since he last set foot in that cemetery, and it seemed of an entirely different quality than he remembered. The storied vault sat in the center of an open area, among haphazard rows of cracked and crumbling obelisks. On top of the structure stood the weeping woman, her face wet from the rain so that it appeared almost as if tears were emerging from the rock itself. The vault's heavy, metal door was, strangely, cracked open, but from where Eric stood it was much too dark to see inside.

Boom! He leapt as thunder rumbled through the forest. He clutched his chest at the shock of it and took a knee to adjust his pack and headlamp. He groaned as he got back to his feet. It knew it would be completely dark before he got back to his car, and he began to really regret the journey. But Eric put aside his doubts after looking at his phone and seeing that he was almost to the GPS point. He was surprised that it appeared to signal that the cache was located within, or near, the vault itself!

Eric's headlamp illuminated a fresh set of footprints on the forest floor. Heavy boots. He paused and listened. He

53

couldn't believe it. Who else would be out here? This place is abandoned. The damn cache is out of play...

When he heard movement just beyond the vault, he tightened up. He listened for the telltale sounds of someone walking through the woods, but all he heard was the spattering of rain hitting leaves and branches, and the call of a few peepers. He searched the ground and then the surrounding woodline for any additional sign of another person, straining his eyes, scanning into the gloom that now enveloped him in that lonely, forgotten cemetery.

"Hillary!" he called out, then shrunk back, unsure of why he had shouted her name. Still, he looked for her there, anticipating her long blond hair, her blue windbreaker, emerging from the forest.

After giving up on finding anyone, he checked his phone again. The blue dot was still just ahead, blinking right where the vault was located. Here we go! He wasn't superstitious about graveyards, but the dreary weather, coupled with his curiosity over the fresh tire and boot marks, made him anxious.

Eric stepped slowly toward the mausoleum. His boots made nasty sucking sounds as he plodded through the mucky soil, and the rainwater only accentuated the strong, weedy odor of the grounds. Then he heard it. It was unmistakable. A faint sobbing from inside the vault. He stopped before the green-tinged metal door and looked up at the weeping figure which adorned the mausoleum. His heart beat erratically and his mouth parched instantly. When he placed his palm against the door, the wind whipped up, and the crying ceased.

"Hillary?" Eric had said it quietly, just above a whisper. He considered the possibility that while he was tromping through the forest, she had driven around the barrier and had beaten him to the cemetery. He had to know.

Although the door to the vault was already ajar, Eric had to put effort into widening it so that he could fit inside. He held his breath as he stepped inside. The interior was, as he expected, in horrible disrepair. His headlamp illuminated the

54

narrow chamber and he saw piles of loose rock, broken wood, and some animal bones. No sobbing woman nor ghoul occupied the vault, to his relief. But what captured his attention was an army-green ammunition box set in one corner. It was the cache!

The thrill of finding it provided Eric some immediate relief from his taxing journey and was a much-needed distraction from the unsettling tenor of the cemetery. He grinned as he pressed his thumbs on the latches and lifted the lid. Inside the box he found a plastic zip-lock bag containing a folded piece of paper. There was no logbook, which disappointed him. He wanted to sign his name, make it known that he had been one of the few, perhaps the last, to make the trip.

Eric opened the bag and removed the paper, his heart thumping wildly with anticipation. He had sacrificed so many hours over the years to his hobby—it had always been worth the squeeze to him—the adventure was a reward in and of itself. Unfolding the paper, which turned out to be a rose-decorated stationery, he revealed a short, written message. The handwriting was intimately familiar.

Eric,

By the time you read this, I'll have moved in with Luke. We've been seeing each other for months, not that I ever expected you to notice. I've tried, and failed, to keep your attention for years. Ultimately, you have your hobbies and interests, and they make you happier than I ever could dream to.

I truly hope you find whatever it is you're looking for out there.
—Hillary

When Eric dropped the note, his lamplight reflected off a small, metallic object remaining within the bag. It was a cache like no other, that was true, for inside was a priceless treasure: Hillary's wedding ring.

The House on Pearl Ave

The little yellow house on Pearl Avenue had seen several families come and go in its sixty-year existence, but Simon Dutter was currently its sole occupant. He inhabited one of the home's three quaint bedrooms, and with as few pieces of furniture as he had, much of the wall and floor space was left bare. Whenever he entered the house, he was reminded of his marital status; his footsteps would echo interminably, no decorative furniture or furnishings, no loveseats, toys, or other evidence of a family unit to fill (and fulfill) the space.

Reminders of past inhabitants couldn't be ignored. A notched dining room door frame documented the growth of a Judy, side by side with her several-inches-taller brother, Daniel. Within a bedroom closet, Simon found a cigar box full of arrowheads and baseball cards. Outside, on the porch, sat a two-person swing with two names carved into the oak: Esther and Reggie.

Feelings of regret and a self-loathing over missed opportunities had become more and more potent as Simon entered his thirties. The idea of sharing the space with a wife and child, of building a family, appealed to him, at least in theory. In practice, however, he had long given up the pursuit of familial bliss. Simon, ten years on, was still crippled by the breakup with his college girlfriend, Kiki. They had dated for three years and, without thinking of the reality of their professional dreams and blinded by their earnest, inexperienced love, had discussed marriage. But they talked about it in a flippant, romanticized way—Simon had never proposed, and she had never asked him to. When they

57

graduated, the relationship deteriorated in the most natural of ways. Simon wanted to stay one more year at Binghampton College to complete his master's, but Kiki wished to leave Binghampton in pursuit of a professional position in Brooklyn. They tried to make it work, talking on the phone every night for months, but Kiki had already moved on, and long before she had ever left for the city.

Ten years can pass quickly in a driven life. Marriage and kids are meant to slow it all down, force a person to wade in the thick of it for years, as they service the needs of others before their own. Simon couldn't recall much of his twenties. He became a team supervisor at an engineering firm at 28, and was eventually scooped up and placed into middle management at a local software company as he eclipsed thirty.

He and Kiki ran into each other from time to time around Binghampton, as both their families were from the area. He had never called or sent her embarrassing emails after their emotional, yet rational breakup; he maintained some level of restraint, despite his longing. But he demonstrated his inability to move on through his isolation and refusal to pursue other women. When Simon wasn't at work, he was at home. Days quickly become weeks, weeks become months, and he remained as he was, with few passions or hobbies to speak of.

Hardly anything of note had occurred in Simon's life for quite some time, when he bumped into Kiki at the Wegmans supermarket one sunny spring day. A blue-eyed toddler with a full mane of dark brown hair sat in her shopping cart.

"Hey, Kiki!" said Simon, beaming.

"Simon! How are you?" she replied, hugging him.

"I'm good. Wow, so who's the little one?" He already knew the answer, as he had followed Kiki on Facebook since their breakup. He had watched her move on—a self-torment nearly in real time, dissecting the countless selfies she posted as she went out clubbing with her new girlfriends. He recognized the small clues when she began dating again, and knew the moment she became serious with a guy named Mark, by way of her digital declaration of the newly minted relationship status. Simon found a brief respite from his voyeuristic self-flagellation when the couple broke up for a few weeks, and he found a brief joy in her renunciation of all relations with men and mankind. He was crushed when pictures of her and Mark's reunion began appearing on Kiki's Facebook feed.

As time passed, Simon accepted that Kiki and Mark's marriage was inevitable, and felt no ill will in witnessing second-hand the joy of their union, or upon reading the couple's subsequent pregnancy announcement. At some point, Simon had grown up, and it made him genuinely happy to see how Kiki had changed with the birth of her daughter, Keeley. It didn't feel right anymore to be jealous at the joy of others. He accepted that he could have taken a path that paralleled Kiki's, that he had chosen—rightly and rationally—to pursue his own career.

Kiki introduced Simon to Keeley, and the former couple talked for a few minutes, catching up. Simon didn't have much to share beyond his new job, and how terrible his allergies had been that spring, reiterating old news—that his cat, Joules, had passed away the fall prior. Kiki congratulated him on his new job, and again offered him her condolences regarding the cat she had come to know well during their time living together. She then told him a chapter's worth of her rich, exquisite life before the conversation faded into an awkward, though warm, goodbye.

Simon returned home without finishing his shopping. He felt utterly alone in that house. Despite their pleasant exchange, his run-in with Kiki had magnified his exceptional feeling of loss. The encounter was a bitter reminder of his inability to accomplish the things in life that make a man whole: a loving partner, children... He rarely regretted the decision itself—to play it safe and stay in Binghampton. Normally his regret was less concrete. But that afternoon,

Simon knew positively, that he had let the one truly exceptional element in his life slip away.

He had a panic attack of sorts on his leather couch, burying his head in a pillow, groaning without crying, trying not to hyperventilate. Simon even considered contacting Kiki, just to let her know that he had been wrong all those years ago. But he managed to restrain himself and did not make that awkward phone call. That would be a step too far, and he was still self-aware enough, even in his anguish, to realize the burden he would be placing on Kiki. As his ragged breathing ebbed and his heart rate diminished, he sat up and relaxed, and attempted to analyze the way in which his feelings were overwhelming his rational mind.

Simon meditated on an empty wall in his living room as he sunk back into his expensive couch, a couch clearly unsuitable for a home with young children. Long minutes drew out before him during his concentrated effort to put his world to right. But his contemplative moment was soon undermined by the manifestation of an image—a shadowed outline in the shape of a person.

Simon startled, shook his head and looked away, attempting to dismiss this waking dream. He rubbed his irritated eyes, wondering if perhaps his vision had been distorted by his allergies. But this wasn't a case of play between light and shadow in a dark room, and to his amazement, when he looked again in the direction of the once barren wall, there *was* someone standing there—if only the idea of a someone, the thing-in-itself.

Simon sat up and squinted at the nebulous form, and like a camera aperture, the being before him came into focus. It was a woman! Her hair was red, pinned up, and she was wearing a green, floral-printed dress that exemplified 1960s domestic chic.

"Who are you?" he asked, breathlessly, his tongue tracing the roof of his parched mouth. But the woman made no reply, nor did she seem to observe his presence. She merely walked across the room and sat down in an orange-upholstered teak wood chair which, until a moment before, had not actually been manifest in Simon's living room. He moved to get up—whether to flee the room, or just investigate, he wasn't certain—and as he stood, the woman and the chair vanished as quickly as they had appeared.

Simon nervously walked the house, searching for any hint of the woman or the mysterious chair, questioning his senses and his state of mind. He had been having a fit before he spied the silhouette, and he considered that he might have simply imagined the woman. But why was it so detailed—her dress, that radiant hair? Maybe he had seen her at the supermarket or on TV. Or maybe it was just a concocted imagining, a delusion thrown together from disparate sources.

The following days drifted by without further spectral anomaly. Simon's run-in with Kiki no longer weighed on his mind. He had spent most of his time, and allocated the bulk of his intellectual efforts, trying to understand, and attempting to reimagine, or conjure, the red-haired woman in his living room. He tried drifting off to sleep facing the wall where she had appeared; he tried exercising to boost his heart rate, attempting to recreate the fatigue that he had been experiencing at the time of the initial sighting. But none of his experiments coaxed anything out of the ordinary from the environment, nor from the recesses of his mind.

So fixated was Simon on the phantom, that he tore down the barrier which he had placed between how he felt about Kiki and what he felt appropriate to communicate to her. He needed to share what he was experiencing with someone, and she was the only person who came to mind. He hoped that she might offer insight into his disoriented state, and set him to rights, so to speak; and one lonely, burdensome night, he called her.

"Hey, Simon," said Kiki.

"Hi, Kiki. I hope I'm not bothering you."

"No, not at all. Hold on a minute." The line went quiet and Simon could hear Kiki tell her daughter to sit still on the couch. "Sorry. What's going on?"

"Okay, this is going to sound really weird…" Simon explained the situation with the strange woman, all too aware that he had the potential of coming off as unhinged, and worse, needy. But Kiki listened without judgment.

"That is weird," she said, playfully. "Maybe it's a ghost. Do you know if someone died in your house?"

Simon smiled to himself, recalling Kiki's general openness and good nature. "Not that I know of."

"You should ask around your neighborhood. Maybe someone there knows something." Kiki laughed at the thought of it. "You probably received an official deed or abstract that names everyone who has owned your house."

"That's actually a great idea!" He paused, considering whether he should express himself, despite his best judgment. "It's nice talking to you, Kiki. I knew I'd be able to tell you and you wouldn't think I was some kind of weirdo or something."

"You might still be a weirdo. You did see a ghost *and* a ghost *chair*," she said, laughing. "But it's good to catch up, Simon." She paused to scold her daughter for attempting something dangerous. "I'm sorry, she's climbing the bookcase. I should probably go…"

"Before you hang up, I just want to tell you how awful I feel for how things went down between us." Simon then held his breath, and his temples began pulsating.

"Oh, Simon… It all played out how it was supposed to, and we don't hate each other!"

"I should have been more open. I was so focused on getting my master's and doing 'what I was supposed to,' I couldn't see what was right in front of me."

"Really, we're good…"

He continued, impassioned. "You deserved better. You're a great girl, Kiki. I wish I could go back and relive some things. I would have gone with you to New York, and we could've given it a real shot. I knew that we were meant for each other at the time—actually, I still do…"

"Simon, I gotta go. My girl is off the wall," she said, the cheeriness gone from her voice.

"...Okay."

Kiki hung up and all was again silent in Simon's living room. He immediately felt ashamed for making her feel uncomfortable with his inappropriate declaration. He wandered to his bedroom and wept inconsolably.

Simon was pulled from his introspective fit when he caught movement in the mirror over his antique dresser. He watched, breathless, as the woman with the red hair entered the room. Hoping to get a good look at her, he whipped around, but saw no such woman in the doorway. Yet, when he returned his attention to the mirror, she was there as before!

The woman wore a dark dress, but there was nothing discernibly ghastly about her, as one might expect from such a vision. Simon wasn't frightened by her sudden appearance this time around. In fact, he found her oddly charming, in spite of her intrusion into his grieving moment.

As before, she carried on with her tasks, oblivious to his presence. She paused in front of the mirror above his cedar dresser, which the home's previous occupants had left behind. Simon could see she was crying as she touched up her makeup. He felt for this woman, despite not knowing her name or her plight, and strangely wished to console her in some way.

Simon lay back in bed, fixated on the woman in the looking glass. In adjusting his position, he caught her attention. She startled at first, and turned to address the interloper in her room. Finding no one, she paused, as though she was considering what was taking place. When she turned her attention back to the mirror, she seemed to have come to the same conclusion as Simon—that the specter in the room could be found only in its reflection.

Both Simon and the mysterious woman watched each other through the glass. He was enthralled by her. She was stunning, evocative—and despite her tears, she seemed full of

63

life to him. She broke the trance by lifting her hand, leaning toward the mirror from the other side, beckoning to him.

Simon stood, now dry-eyed, and ready for whatever would transpire. He wanted to touch her hand, her face, to make some sort of contact with her. He was somehow confident. It felt right to him; it was as if she was waiting for *him*. Simon didn't think about the 'how' or the 'why,' and in that moment, he didn't care.

No sooner had his feet hit the carpet than his phone rang obtrusively in his pants pocket, and with that interruption, the woman in the mirror abruptly vanished. Simon rushed to the dresser and searched the mirror, running his hands up and down it as if to find the source, a way of reaching the other side and the red-haired woman. But he saw only his own reflection: a 32-year-old man with light-blue eyes and an uninteresting, though classic, side-parted hairstyle.

His phone continued to ring, and, frustrated, he dug it out to see who had interrupted him. It was Kiki. He answered it without hesitation, as seeing her name and picture pop up onscreen triggered feelings, endorphins, and memories. He had been so distracted by his contact with the red-haired woman that he had temporarily forgotten about their last, awkward, conversation.

"Hello?"

"Simon, it's me," said Kiki.

"Hi…"

"Are you busy?"

"No." Simon looked at the mirror again. Nothing. The woman was gone, faded, and Kiki had taken her place in the swelling tide in his conscious mind.

"I just wanted to call and apologize for how short I was with you. You were being honest and baring your heart to me, and I kinda blew you off."

"You don't have to apologize, Kiki. I'm the one who should be sorry." Simon's breath quickened. He felt remorse for dumping his feelings on her and was having trouble swallowing his nerves. "I- I won't ever do anything like that again."

"Oh, Simon…" said Kiki. The line went silent for a few moments before she continued: "I never know what to say. I think about what might have been sometimes, too. But I'm really happy with what I have now."

"I saw my ghost again!" blurted Simon. "This time she was in the mirror in my room—and she saw *me* too!"

"Really? And you have no idea who lived in your house before you?"

"No. I was sure I'd never see her again," said Simon. "But she saw me, and it almost seemed like she wanted to talk." Simon wanted to tell Kiki how the red-haired woman had beckoned to him, how he wished to join her in her world in the mirror and leave behind his dull life in Lestershire. "I'm definitely going to look through the house papers today."

"It's really neat. I love the idea of spirits reliving their lives, trying to contact people to get things done and make things right," said Kiki. "Maybe you can help her in some way. You really should ask some of the older folks around your neighborhood."

Simon chuckled. "I don't know about all that. I think it's more happenstance than anything else. The ghost is probably just going about her business, and I happened to catch her eye at the right time." Simon didn't want to believe that. "But I'm certainly motivated now to do some research, and I'm going to take your advice and start asking around about past residents."

The conversation continued cordially, covering the gamut of light topics: work, family, mutual acquaintances. Simon and Kiki were destined to be long-term friends, and no slip-up nor ill-timed outburst would permanently undermine their connection.

The next day, Simon paged through his thick deed and property records at the desk in his bedroom. The house had passed hands four times since its construction. There were the Johnstons—Timothy and Frida, the first inhabitants of the newly built home in 1959; then Glen McDougal, not long after, in 1962; Mr. and Mrs. Finch in 1975; and Timothy and Judy Gilroy in 2002, who sold it to Simon. He had names, but no way of telling a phantom Finch from a spectral Johnston. That would take some digging.

Pearl Ave. had seen its heyday decades ago. It was now a neighborhood of affordable housing for low-income families ready to take on their first starter homes. Simon's neighbors were younger, many with small children. He left the house and walked down the block to the Oasis for a bite to eat and some time to think.

He would have to find an elderly neighbor, someone who had lived on the street, possibly since they were a kid. But Simon couldn't think of anyone who lived nearby who might be older than sixty. Even the Oasis was full of younger people, though he knew by the menu and vintage furnishings that it had stood the test of time, and seen generations pass through—possibly even the woman with the red hair.

The owner of the bar, Lynn, was the one who served up his hot pie and beer. She was older, and he asked her about the neighborhood.

"We lived next door to the bar here when I was a kid, then moved to a house on Myrtle, just the next street over," said Lynn. "I *knew* plenty of people that lived on Pearl, but the kids I grew up with all moved away. Twenty years ago, the whole neighborhood was sixty-plus. Of course, they all just about moved on, too." She winked at Simon, then went back to the kitchen.

Simon finished his meal and was about to leave when Lynn stopped him at the door.

"Hey, I just remembered—Mrs. Ellsic used to live on Pearl, before her husband died. She lives at the top of the hill now, a few streets to the west, beside Sunshire Cemetery."

"Oh great, could you give me her address?" asked Simon.

66

"Yes… But she can be a bit…prickly," said Lynn, grimacing in a way that made Simon worry. "If she's outside, I'd say go ahead and introduce yourself and talk to her. But I wouldn't knock on her front door or go on her porch."

"I understand. Thank you!"

Lynn wrote down the address and handed it to Simon, reiterating that the old woman might bite his head off if he didn't catch her at the right time of day.

Simon headed out. It was still early, he thought. He would walk up the hill and pay Mrs. Ellsic a visit.

Mrs. Ellsic's grey stucco sat near a cemetery that Simon had only driven past a handful of times. The cemetery was overgrown, derelict, and featured an Eastern-European-style wooden chapel, which had also seen better days. When he came up the front path, he spotted an aged woman with unkempt, white hair, sweeping a side porch. She reminded him of a troll doll, with her wild hair and diminutive stature.

"Hello, my name's Simon. Are you Mrs. Ellsic?"

The old woman looked up and crinkled her nose at the intruder. "No soliciting!"

Simon's mouth went dry and he tensed up. "Ma'am, I'm a neighbor. I live on Pearl Avenue and someone said you might be able to help me."

"I haven't lived there for ages."

He kept his distance. "I own the little yellow house. Number fifty. Do you remember it?"

She eyed him conspicuously. "I know it."

"I'm researching its history, so to speak; do you remember a woman who lived there, with red hair?"

Mrs. Ellsic shrugged, having had enough of the interloper. "I'm not the town historian, son." She made a brushing motion at him with her hand and then the broom.

Simon didn't dare try and continue the conversation. He turned and practically jogged back home, just to get out of her eyesight.

67

The identity of his shadowy houseguest remained a mystery for Simon. Had the woman not been so striking, he might have felt alarmed, frightened, but she was disarming, even *alluring*. Though he had only seen her briefly, he couldn't forget her pretty face and sad eyes; especially not that ravishing red hair.

She was on his mind as he showered one Saturday morning. His work week had been slow, dull beyond words, the sort that made him wonder whether he had chosen the wrong profession. He had nothing going on, nothing to look forward to, at work or at home, and the visions of the red-haired woman, however strange and otherworldly, had been a point of excitement amid the doldrums of his daily life.

The room was thick with steam when Simon stepped out of the shower. As he toweled off, his eyes were drawn to the now-opaque antique mirror in the bedroom. Odd, he thought; he must have been in the shower for quite some time. He drifted out of the *en suite* bathroom and toward his mahogany dresser. Slowly, a vertical line appeared on the dresser mirror, revealing his arm in the reflection. He considered whether it was simply a natural effect of the steam dissipating, until he saw another line appear on the glass, this one horizontal, followed by another vertical line, parallel to the first. "H." He stood, transfixed, as more letters appeared on the glass in succession: E, L, L, O.

It had to be the woman, he thought. He looked for her desperately through the vapor, for her reflection in the mirror, but not enough of the glass was revealed for him to properly 'see' into *her* bedroom.

More words appeared: *I MISS YOU*, followed by *STAY WITH ME*. The condensation was already dissipating, and the messages were fading. Simon quickly took his finger to the glass, and wrote his reply: *WHO ARE YOU?*

Not long after he dotted the question mark, the messages vanished, save for a faint trace of his own message. A long minute passed. Simon waited for a response, searching the mirror, and sweating in the thick, sticky heat left over from the shower. "Tell me your name," he said. "Reveal yourself." But he would get no answer, not after ten minutes, not after twenty.

He spent the remainder of the morning trying to entice further communication with his spectral cohabitant, cooling his room then running the shower to recreate the foggy mirror, and repeating the process until he had run out of hot water.

Frustrated, Simon smacked the mirror, breaking one of the rear braces and causing it to tilt slightly. He pulled out each drawer, ripping out his clothes, as if he were searching for the woman inside the dresser itself. The bottom drawer was the last to go and was a real hassle to remove from its track. With a loud grunt, Simon yanked the drawer out, splitting its rear panel in two.

He sat down in his pile of clothes, among the dresser drawers, emotionally exhausted. It was then that he spotted a black-and-white photograph that had been tucked in the rear of that bottom drawer; stuck, likely missed by one of the antique's earliest owners. The photo was that of a man of about thirty with dark hair, wearing a cardigan and collared shirt.

Simon pulled out the picture and stood up. When he flipped it over he spotted a name and year: *Reggie '60*. "I'll be damned... Reggie and *Esther*." He immediately thought of the front porch swing and the couple's names carved into it. What were the chances that Reggie's Esther was the woman in his mirror? Or was it Esther's mirror?

He looked through his deed again but found no evidence of a Reggie or Esther. The owners in 1960 were Timothy and Frida Johnston, followed by a man named Glen a few years later.

He was determined to find out who Reggie and Esther were, now that he had a photo, and there was only one person he knew of that could help him.

Simon arrived at the old stucco home early in the afternoon that Saturday. The sky was overcast, the weather cool and miserable. He didn't see Mrs. Ellsic dawdling about the property, so he went right up to the front door and knocked. Following a minute of nervous anticipation, the heavy interior door opened, while the metal screen door remained shut. The elderly woman seemed to peek out of the shadows from her dark house.

"You again? What do you want?"

"Good afternoon, ma'am. My name's Simon, in case you've forgotten." Simon inhaled sharply, before continuing: "I found a picture in an antique dresser of mine. I'm hoping you might recognize the man in it."

"Why? Who cares?"

Before she could turn away and slam the door in his face, he placed the photo against the screen door. Mrs. Ellsic couldn't help but glimpse the picture, and when she did she paused for a moment. Simon saw her heavy, morose expression lighten considerably.

"Lord. I haven't thought of Reggie in forty years," said Mrs. Ellsic, breaking the silence. "Such a dear man. He cut my grass for me after my own husband passed."

"So, you knew Esther, too?"

"Certainly. We were close until she moved back to her parents' home on the southside."

Mrs. Ellsic unlocked and cracked the screen door so she could get a better look at the old photograph. She eyed the picture, then looked Simon over. "Are you a Johnston? Sure do look a bit like Reginald."

"Oh, no. Not that I know of, anyway," said Simon, amazed at how warm Mrs. Ellsic had become since seeing the old photo. "Esther and Reggie Johnston, then? Do you know who Timothy and Frida Johnston are?"

"Yes. Reggie's parents."

Now Simon was unsure whether or not his ghost might be the mother, Frida. "Did the parents live at fifty Pearl? Who had the red hair?"

70

"You sure do ask a lot of questions," she replied. "No, the parents built the house for Esther and Reggie after they were married. Last I heard, one of the Johnstons was living at Floral nursing home."

"The one by the cemetery?"

Mrs. Ellsic nodded. "I haven't seen any of these people since the early Sixties. You best pay them a visit, as it's none of my business." With that she closed the door and disappeared back inside her dark domicile.

Simon still had so many questions, including the most important one of all. Was Esther the woman with the red hair—his ghostly crush? He returned home and put off a trip to the nursing center. There was too much new information for him to process. He would try and find the relative Mrs. Ellsic spoke of the following day.

When Simon arrived at Floral Nursing and Rehabilitation Center on that Sunday afternoon, things didn't go as smoothly as he had hoped. The nurses thought he was soliciting when he came in asking for a 'Mr. or Mrs. Johnston.' He told them he wasn't family, that he hoped he could talk to the Johnstons about the history of his house on Pearl Avenue.

"Sure thing, guy. What did you say your name was? Simon?" asked the nurse manning the reception desk. "We'll write down your information and give it to Mrs. Johnston. There's no *Mr.* Johnston here."

"Could you tell me Mrs. Johnston's first name, at least?"

The nurse shook her head and pointed toward the door. "Nope. This isn't a public place. This is a residence and it's about time for supper. Good day."

Simon sighed and turned toward the door. Residents had begun milling about, most on their way to the dining room. As he reached the vestibule, he heard a woman call for him to wait. He looked back over his shoulder and shivered when he looked the woman in the eye. She had a shock of red in her mostly white and grey hair.

71

The old woman looked him over as if she'd seen a ghost from her past. "Christ. I thought you were one of Reggie's nephews. My name's Esther." She offered her hand and Simon took it.

"Simon. Are you the Esther Johnston who lived on Pearl Ave.?"

She nodded. "For a little while, anyway."

"This is going to sound crazy, but I think I'm in contact with your mom's spirit—through an antique mirror."

Esther's jaw dropped. She cupped both of Simon's cheeks in her hands and inspected him closely. "I knew I'd seen you before. My goodness, you look just like him."

"Who?" asked Simon.

"My husband, Reggie. He passed away in the early Sixties, and I thought he had been visiting me, watching over me; but it was *you*! Wasn't it?"

"I don't understand, Esther. I've been seeing a ghost, not just in the mirror—I saw a woman with red hair walk through my living room and vanish."

"When I stopped seeing him, I thought he had moved on. I was happy for him. Oh, Simon… You don't understand how much it helped me to move on, to see him again—even if it was just you," said Esther, gently weeping, hugging Simon to her. "I got to say goodbye. He had passed so suddenly. We were only married two years."

It was then that Simon realized that it hadn't been a ghost in his mirror—it really was Esther from decades prior, as she grieved her departed husband. Somehow their heartache had connected them through time—through the mirror.

They sat down and had a long conversation, sharing the stories of their lives, discussing the fantastic nature of their meeting. Simon returned weekly, and he and Esther became close friends. He learned how Esther had remarried and had children after he had appeared in her life. She learned how he had been carrying a torch for Kiki since college, and

72

encouraged him, inspired him, and through her own example, showed him how to move on from tragedy and isolation.

From time to time, Simon and Esther contemplated the 'how' and the 'why' of their coming together. They had theories about what had transpired in that home, regarding their connection nearly six decades apart. Esther wanted to believe in reincarnation. Simon liked to think it was some sort of magic mirror; having heard a local legend about a woman who took her own life after seeing into her future in such a looking glass. He even tried to trace the dresser's history, as Esther said that she and Reggie had bought it used, from a hardware store on Clinton Street. The same store space was now occupied by the son of the hardware store owner who had sold them the piece—a curiosity shop purported to carry hexed, odd, and even macabre items and furniture.

74

With These Rings, I Thee Dread

"This is a symbol of our trust, our devotion to one another," said Martin, as he slid a sterling silver ring with a blue-white opal onto the finger of his longtime girlfriend. The ring was inscribed with intricate Celtic symbols, the meanings of which the antique shop owner had tried to explain, but Martin wasn't all that interested in things like magic and astrology.

"This is so sweet, babe," said Katie, smiling. The couple were seated at a small table in the Indian restaurant at which they had first met. "Your turn." She removed a second, larger, though no less ornate, ring from the small, scarlet box and placed it on Martin's finger, completing the ceremony.

"Now it's official." Martin smiled. The couple had been dating for two years, but he had never felt entirely comfortable. Katie had been faithful for the entirety of their relationship, and showed no signs of doubt or unhappiness, but nonetheless Martin carried with him feelings of inadequacy, fearing that she would eventually leave or be unfaithful. The promise rings that he had purchased, and which Katie, to his relief, fully embraced, offered him a sense of security which he so terribly needed. If he couldn't always be with her physically, at least he could be with her in spirit.

The following morning the happy couple said their goodbyes and headed their separate ways for work. Martin felt especially content, knowing that Katie had left wearing her new promise ring, a constant reminder of him and their inviolable bond, and he didn't much mind pushing papers

75

and fielding dull phone calls that day. He finally had the assurance he so desperately needed.

All was copacetic for Martin until lunchtime. He was seated at his desk, checking his email, when he felt a sudden strange sensation throughout his body. It felt to him as if he had slipped into a dream, but his eyes were wide open and he was still very much conscious of his surroundings. The concurrent dream imagery in his mind's eye was vague, murky, but the focal point was crystal clear: *Katie*. There she was, clear as day, wearing the very blue blouse and brown skirt in which she had left the house. She was walking up the steps of a building downtown that he was sure he had seen before. When she reached the top, the door opened and a handsome man in a suit stepped outside, greeting her with a smile. Katie then followed the man inside and the door closed behind them, Martin taking the whole scene in as if he were watching a fuzzy TV show.

As the vision faded and his office cubicle again became the sole setting for his conscious mind, Martin's eyes were drawn to a faint light emanating from his hand. The promise ring was glowing softly upon his finger, as if it had been just pulled from a hot mold. He checked to make sure it wasn't a simple reflection from the overhead fluorescent lights. He only noticed it a few seconds before the glow faded and the ring was once again an ordinary silver band around his finger.

Martin brooded over the vision. Why would his mind concoct such an uncomfortable scene? It had seemed as real as the clicks of his keyboard, the conversations of his coworkers. He had even heard the door opening, the timbre of Katie's voice, some light street noise. The man in the vision was certainly attractive, and the doubt that Martin had grown all too familiar with burrowed its way back into his brain. *What if Katie really is seeing another man right now?* he wondered. *What if she's not at work?* He contemplated the scenario before writing the whole thing off as a simple daydream and returned to his work.

As the couple ate dinner at home that evening, Martin asked Katie what she had been up to that day.

"Nothing special. We did some mandatory training with HR in the morning. Bev and I went to Mangialardo's for lunch, and the rest of the afternoon I mostly browsed Facebook."

"Oh, so you didn't go *downtown* at all?" asked Martin, smiling awkwardly. Mangialardo's was located on the city's west side, a good walk away from Binghampton's business district.

Katie paused. "Why do you think I would go downtown?"

"I don't know...I thought maybe you'd go shopping today. It was nice out."

"You know I'd love to. But I've really got to make a dent in my student loans. The credit card debt, too."

"You're right." Martin decided to end his investigation, considering the absurdity of it all, and he and Katie spent the rest of the evening discussing prospects for their future.

Martin was at his desk the next day, taking his lunch, when he again felt the curious sensation from the day before, this time coupled with a new vision. Again, he saw Katie, wearing the outfit he had seen her in that morning, but this time she was with a different man. He was tall, a little older, with a well-groomed moustache, no less attractive than the man from the first daydream. The man and Katie were walking down a city sidewalk, smiling and chatting. Their conversation was muffled, but it was clearly a pleasant one, evidenced by their upbeat tone and occasional laughter.

Boooooooong! Martin jerked in his seat at the sound of church bells outside his building, so wrapped up was he in his vision. He was taken aback that Katie and the man seemed to be reacting to the bells also, looking up toward what Martin assumed to be an unseen belfry.

The thought was ludicrous—that he was envisioning Katie's actions in real-time—but that didn't prevent him from

77

calling her just to see what she was up to. Sure enough, the Katie in his concurrent vision removed her phone from her purse. She looked at the screen for a couple seconds, but, rather than answer it, returned it to her purse and resumed her conversation with the man.

As the scene faded, Martin again noticed the promise ring emitting a strange glow, as if it and the visions he was experiencing were connected in some way. He nervously tapped his feet, taking it all in. Maybe it was real, maybe Katie *was* seeing other men. A crushing nausea consumed him then, and he ran to the bathroom to vomit. When he had voided the contents of his lunch, he washed his hands and looked into the mirror above the sink. He was not an obese man, but certainly not as fit or genetically gifted as the men in his visions. Even in his dress shirt and slacks, there was a certain shabbiness to his appearance that made him wonder if he, a temporary data entry clerk, was really a quality partner for Katie.

Weeks passed, and Martin's doubts only intensified. The visions continued, and he "watched" as Katie met multiple times a week with the same men. As always, the images were distorted, but it was clear that Katie and the men were becoming more comfortable with each other. He never witnessed any physical interaction between Katie and his rivals—that, he assumed, happened behind closed doors. But all that changed one afternoon when he saw his girlfriend and the mustachioed man embrace. It wasn't gratuitous, but it incensed Martin to no end. He was no longer able to subdue the torment and rage which consumed him on a near-daily basis. He thought about taking the promise ring off and putting the visions to an end, but it was too tempting. He knew Katie was up to something, and he felt a strong compulsion to follow her and catch her in the act.

The next time the ring glowed, he was ready. The vision began, as usual, at midday. Again, Katie met with the man with the moustache, and again the church bells rang both in dreamlife and in reality. Rather than sit and stew in worry, Martin left his office. He ran down the sidewalks of downtown Binghampton, following the sound of the bells, combing the streets for Katie and her new companion.

He stopped mid-run when he saw them. There stood Katie, in front of the First Presbyterian Church, with the very man that, until that point, Martin had only envisioned. It was all *real*. Again, she hugged the man and said goodbye, and the two went their separate ways.

Martin thought about confronting Katie then, but instead followed the man, who left the sun-drenched sidewalk and entered the confines of a dimly lit parking complex. Martin followed him down to a lower level, maintaining a considerable distance, so as to conceal himself, taking slow, measured steps to muffle the echo of his dress shoes.

Before the man could get into his car, Martin leapt and tackled him. He unleashed all his pent-up rage on the man, strangling him. All the self-hatred from years of burying his feelings of inadequacy was redirected outward, and through his hands; the hands that throttled a stranger. Martin could hear a cracking in the man's neck and felt the man's body crumple beneath him.

He had no time to process the enormity of his deed, however, as the promise ring glowed and he was again granted second sight of Katie. To his disgust, he saw her with a third man, unfamiliar, this one cleanly shaven and wearing a slim-fitting suit. The two were walking into the lobby of the Clinton St. Hotel, not two blocks away from the parking complex.

He released the stranger, staring at his bruised neck and expressionless face, briefly shuddering, before running out of the complex to confront Kate.

Minutes later, he arrived at the hotel, charging through the front doors.

"*Martin*?!" said Katie, who stood in the lobby, next to the cleanly shaven man.

Martin stared breathlessly at the pair, his fists clenched.

"Martin?" said the man. "This is...*Martin?*" He grinned as if he were pleasantly surprised.

"What are you doing here, Marty? How did you know?"

Martin held up his hand and pointed to the promise ring, which still glowed faintly. "Do you see this? This is a symbol of my love for you, Katie. Is yours just some meaningless piece of metal to you?" He lurched closer, and the other man began to back away. "I know you've been with other men. I've seen you. You *whore*. Who is this guy?"

Katie's bemused expression faded, replaced by a disbelieving scowl. "What the hell are you talking about?! This is Garrett. He's a professional party planner. I've been working with him to plan a surprise birthday party for you, asshole." Tears streamed down her now-trembling face.

"You liar. I've seen you...." But Martin had no more time to explain, as the police ran through the doors to arrest him for the murder of Reverend Ryan Owens, whom Katie had been meeting with to discuss wedding plans for her and Martin. Her testimony would later reveal that the first man she was meeting with was a financial planner with Farrell Dench, through which she was attempting to take care of her personal debt, all in dedication to her and Martin's future together.

Mr. Green's Passional

The greenhouse was substantial and could be seen by any motorist travelling Stella Ireland Road. Many assumed it housed a commercial enterprise, though there was no sign, nor any advertisement around the Green property, hinting that business took place there. The greenhouse sat just behind a little yellow house, the home where Paul Green had grown up, the one his parents had built in their first year of marriage in the late 1970s.

Now Mr. and Mrs. Green were long dead, and Paul was a moderately successful academic—an associate professor of botany and cellular biology at Binghampton College. He lived alone, had never married, never really dated, and preferred the company of plants, specifically flowering vines and rare orchids, to that of his fellow sentient creatures. He was on a year-long sabbatical from the college, busy working on genetic hybridization, and hadn't seen any of his colleagues for some time. So, Paul was taken aback when his closest acquaintance from the college, Dr. Tomasita Gonzalez, appeared at the entrance to his greenhouse.

"Dr. Gonzalez?" Paul called out, as he made his way through the lush green and vibrant blossoming hues to meet his guest. He was exceptionally nervous as he opened the sturdy glass door to let Tomasita in. He briefly caught his reflection, and was relieved that he had shaved that morning, and that there was no dirt or grime on his face from his daylong labor.

"So, *this* is the greenhouse?" said Tomasita. "It's very impressive, Paul."

81

"Thanks. You're welcome to have a look around." He turned away, anxious about what she would think of his work. He recognized Dr. Gonzalez's beauty, her supreme evolutionary fitness, but he was also very aware that he felt no attraction toward her—as he had likewise felt no romantic feeling toward any human being up to that point in his life. He knew she paid special attention to him, and that any of the other male professors would relish having Tomasita poking her nose into their research at their private residences.

She carried herself with elegance, as she sauntered down the rows of vegetation in her high heels and smart, knee-length skirt. She paused briefly in front of Paul's pet project and source of pride, as if she could already tell the significance of his unpublished breakthrough on sight alone. "Is that *Hydnora africana*?"

Paul was impressed that she hadn't batted an eye at the stench which the *africana* emitted. "Yes, of course," stated Paul, as he scurried to show her its root system, which was intertwined with that of an incredibly rare orchid. "And I believe I have the only example of a carnivorous orchid at hand!" He said it with such an overzealous, strikingly unprofessional glee, that Tomasita couldn't help but cringe. Luckily, she was leaning in for a better look at the orchid, so Paul hadn't caught sight of her fleeting grimace.

"I don't believe it. These hoods capture insects? They certainly look *familiar*." Tomasita turned her head and grinned, stroking the pink faux-labia of the orchid, as Paul blushed. The flowers certainly resembled female genitalia, which Paul could appreciate, if only aesthetically.

"Y- yes, of course, and not just insecta." Paul had caught on to her flirtation, but it wasn't in his nature to flirt back. He went and retrieved a box which was marked by holes, and took out an undersized deer mouse.

Tomasita gasped as Paul dropped the critter into the four-inch-deep throat of the orchid. The lip almost immediately sealed itself, as if the flower were a closing fist.

She only then noticed the small, prickly spines surrounding the lips of the closed hood.

"The digestive enzymes must be quite potent," stated Tomasita.

"Yes, quite. There's a third element here. I don't know if you can tell, but the *africana* is also utilizing a hybrid of *Nepenthes*—see the climbing stem?" Paul pointed out the parasitic interplay between the orchid, putrid *africana*, and the *Nepenthes*.

"This is incredible, Paul," said Tomasita, impressed by her frumpy, oddly handsome colleague. "The orchid is utilizing the tropical pitcher plant's digestive fluid and hooded structure—and the parasitic *africana* is the reason this is all possible?"

"Yes! It's all very exciting, Dr. Gonzalez," said Paul, beaming with pride as he lovingly stroked one of the lips of the orchid. "And she's not done growing!"

Tomasita put her hand on her colleague's shoulder. "Please, Paul, call me Tom. We've known each other for years now."

He flinched when she slowly slid her hand down to his elbow.

"You look like you haven't eaten in days, dear. How about we got out for a late lunch and you tell me more about your hybrid?"

Paul feigned a smile as he backed away. "I'm sorry, Dr. Gonzalez; maybe another time? I'm very busy with my research."

Tomasita crinkled her nose, then turned abruptly, surprising Paul, and strutted toward the exit.

"Goodbye!" Paul called out to her, unsure whether or not he had offended her.

Tomasita certainly wasn't used to being turned down for lunch dates, or anything else for that matter, but she knew her friend was socially awkward, and gave him the benefit of the doubt. "I'll see you around, Paul. Call me if you wanna go out for a drink sometime." She had said it without looking back.

The door snapped shut behind her, and Paul was again alone with his closest companions.

Weeks later, late one evening, Paul found himself back at the college, searching for a special nutrient that he had run out of at home. His flowering, carnivorous hybrid was consuming much more of the rare nitrate, and he needed to 'borrow' some from the laboratory he shared with Tomasita and another professor, Dr. Stewart. However, while he had found a full container of his plant food additive, he was stopped by Dr. Stewart in the hallway outside of the lab.

"Paul, you can't take that. You know how tight our budget is this year," stated Dr. Stewart, a man who most often presented himself as Paul's professional rival.

"Of course, the budget. I will be glad to speak with the Chair and work out a reimbursement..." said Paul, nervously.

Dr. Stewart grabbed the container and attempted to pry it from Paul's hands, but Paul held tight. Paul was shocked and panicking, astounded that he was being physically confronted over plant food. But he wasn't willing to let his hybrid go unfed.

"Dr. Green, it is out of the question. You can't take something from the lab before it is accounted for," said Dr. Stewart. "You must go through the proper channels—especially when on sabbatical."

But before the argument could escalate, Tomasita had appeared in the hallway and was marching toward the confrontation. "*Professors*, what is going on here?!"

Dr. Stewart released his hold on the container and stepped back. "Dr. Gonzalez, I merely came upon our colleague taking supplies, and attempted to refresh him on the proper channels for utilizing college property."

"What do you need, Paul?"

Paul didn't immediately reply, but handed Tomasita the container, afraid that she too would chastise him.

"This is for your *Hydnora* hybrid?"

"Yes. I fully intended to leave a note..."

Dr. Stewart began to object, but Tomasita shushed him. "I'll sign off on it, Dr. Stewart. I've seen Dr. Green's work in person. It really is *astounding*."

Dr. Stewart practically sneered at Paul as he turned and went into the lab, slamming the door behind him.

"Thanks, Tomasita," mumbled Paul, still shaken after Dr. Stewart's aggressive posturing.

"You look like hell, Paul," stated Tomasita, grinning. "How about you buy me a drink for having your back?"

Paul nodded. He was thankful that she had stepped in when she did and reasoned that he could afford a few hours away from the greenhouse to cultivate their budding relationship.

"The beautiful uniformity and sensual symmetry of the petals, and the attractive properties of color really get to me, Tom," said Paul. His cheeks were flushed, as he was mildly inebriated after two beers at the Oasis.

"*Haha*! Dr. Green! You talk of your orchids as if they were a variety of womankind," replied Tomasita, placing her hand on his wrist, which rested on the bar.

Paul paused, but didn't retract his hand, and let a tense silence fall between them as they drank. He knew that Tomasita was flirting with him, that she was exhibiting all of the signs of a woman who was physiologically interested in a man, and he silently cursed himself that he felt no similar connection. He *did* want to connect with another person, in the same way he felt connected to the things that grew in his greenhouse—to have a lasting intimacy and a confidante to turn to at the end of each day—the idea really appealed to him. Yet, he also regretted that Dr. Gonzalez, the closest living person to him, the only person he would currently consider a friend, had an ulterior motive. It would have been so much easier for him if her intentions were merely those of a friend.

"I'm so close, Dr. Gonzalez...so close," Paul mumbled.

Tomasita smirked at his secrecy regarding some of the more technical aspects of his research, as if she had anything more than a personal interest in Paul's pursuits. "You can tell me, Paul. I can keep a secret."

"You already think I'm a lunatic!" laughed Paul, as he finally removed his hand from beneath Tomasita's. "God, it's just that I've never had a hybrid this fecund, this...*fertile.*"

Tomasita's eyes went wide. "How big has the hybrid gotten?"

Paul looked down the bar, making sure no one else could hear him. "The merging of the three plants is incredible; it's just so naturally elegant."

"What is the depth of the pitcher portion now?"

"Thirty-nine centimeters..."

Tomasita gasped. "That big! I can't believe it!"

Paul put his finger over her mouth. "Keep it down! This plant means the world to me and I don't want anyone poking around my greenhouse."

"Until you publish, right?" asked Tomasita, as she gently lowered his hand from her face. "Dr. Stewart will blow a gasket. You have to publish ASAP."

Paul's expression soured, as Tomasita chuckled to herself at the thought of their dour colleague no longer being the most well-known biologist at the college. "No! I don't want Dr. Stewart, or anyone else, having access to my project," stated Paul, angrily. "This is going to be a generational project. It'll be years before I can release my results."

Tomasita wilted at Paul's sudden change in mood. "Ok, Paul..."

Paul was now growing suspicious—a revelatory insight likely magnified by the influence of the alcohol. "Dr. Gonzalez, why did you come to my greenhouse that day? Was it the Chair, or maybe Dr. Stewart who put you up to checking in on me?"

Tomasita grimaced. "Christ, Paul... I thought we were friends, and I wanted to see you. I knew you were kind of a

86

loner, but now I'm beginning to think that maybe you're just a misanthrope."

Paul stood up, inadvertently knocking the barstool to the floor. "You can tell Stewart and his ilk that they can wait to find out about my research in the *Journal of Plant Biology*, the same as everyone else." He staggered toward the exit, limping slightly from having banged his knee on the barstool as it fell. "Also, stay out of my greenhouse!"

Tomasita didn't reply, shocked at how incensed her colleague had become during an innocent conversation over beer.

The following morning, Tomasita attempted to contact Paul, to see if she could mend their friendship for the sake of their professional relationship and future work environment. She had gone to bed the previous night regretting that she had disparaged him, and wanted to apologize. However, Paul didn't respond to her emails, or to the messages she left on his office voicemail and personal phone.

After her final class that afternoon, Tomasita decided she would stop by Paul's greenhouse and apologize in person. She figured that he would also have a different perspective on their prior night's conflict, as he too had been under the influence at the time. She just hoped that he hadn't been serious when he said that she was barred from visiting him.

Tomasita held her breath as she pushed open the door to the greenhouse. The putrid stench from the *Hydnora* had already concealed the perfumed scents of the multitude of flowers which one first met upon entry. Paul would certainly be in there, thought Tomasita, as his car was in the driveway, and the morning's newspaper was still sitting on the front stoop of the house. Twilight was approaching, but it was not yet dark enough that there would have to be lights on to navigate the greenhouse.

"Paul? Are you here?" Tomasita walked the center aisle, between a menagerie of blooming flowers and hanging vines,

87

before calling out again: "It's Tom. I'm sorry for coming over unannounced, but I really wanted to apologize..."

She shuddered when she saw her friend slumped over on the floor, his pants oddly bunched around his thighs. He lay on his right side, facing away, as Tomasita approached. "Paul!"

She slowly knelt next to the man, then turned him on his back, assuming the worst. His eyes were wide open and missing their small, Promethean spark, and his skin was an ashen gray, cool to the touch.

"Oh, *no, no, no!*" Tomasita leapt to her feet and slowly backed away from the corpse, holding her hand over her mouth and nose as she wept and whispered small prayers for her colleague.

But what had most frightened Tomasita, what she had ultimately reacted to after spotting the pool of blood beneath her friend, and what was now causing a short circuit in her normally methodological thought process, was the fact that Paul's genitals had been severed.

"What have you done, Paul?!" screamed Tomasita, as she followed the streaks and droplets of blood from the small, dark pool on the floor to the garden box which contained the now five-foot-tall, and as broad, amalgam of parasitic *Hydnora*, a tangle of thorny vines, and the now-massive orchid.

She took a few small steps toward the intimidating, enclosed pitcher of the orchid, spying Paul's blood on the colorful labial entrance, or gullet, of the flower's predatory trap. Tomasita attempted to better identify how Paul had been killed by the plant, as it was obviously not a toxic reaction, but a mechanical laceration to the man.

Just as Tomasita attempted to pry the jagged lid of the pitcher open, to verify that her friend's member had indeed been separated by the plant, she felt a strange tugging on her sweater. When she looked down she saw that she had gotten herself snagged on the long thorns of two of the vines. But as she tried to shake herself free, she only caught additional vines on her clothing, some of the thorns even digging into the soft flesh of her forearms and thighs.

Tomasita was astounded as her situation worsened. It was as if the vines were extending themselves toward her, fishing for her. The thorns seemed to pulsate as they pushed through her clothes and into her skin. Then she saw it—that thing which was not sentient, and yet the pilot for the horror which was befalling her. The gaping, serrated maw of the orchid's pitcher slowly opened before her as her body became encircled by the vines.

Now incapacitated, and merely inches away from Paul's creation, Tomasita could identify some of the human remains inside. She thought of her friend as she was pulled closer to that horrendously beautiful, and extremely rare, hybrid— which her colleague had designed, and unbeknownst to her, had fed with his own genetic material.

Her, He, and a Corpse Makes Three

One would not expect a funeral home to be the impetus for a fervid romance, but Tommi Kapowski and Mark Morton were not your typical couple. Though their friends and family found their fascination with death odd, for Tommi and Mark working with the deceased was a privilege. As office assistant at Coleman's Funeral Home, Tommi helped handle the business side of things. Mark, Coleman's embalmer, worked directly with the corpses, forestalling decomposition so that loved ones could see their spouse, parent, or child off as they best remembered them. The bodies they dealt with were the lifeless vessels of *human beings*, people who had loved passionately, lost dearly, accomplished great things, dreamed impossible dreams—not faceless cadavers to turn over for a buck—and the couple bonded over their shared purpose in sending these souls off to the afterlife. Everyone deserved closure, they believed, no matter their age or life circumstances at death.

Tommi and Mark were chatting in the office, which also served as a break room, discussing what they'd do after their dinner date that night, when Mr. Coleman called out from the back of the building.

"Mark, where are you? Let's get a move on it!"

Mark rushed to the back exit, where Mr. Coleman waited with a stretcher, on which rested a body bag.

91

"You didn't hear me buzz you?" asked Mr. Coleman. "I've been standing out here in the rain with this guy for a few minutes now."

"Sorry, I was talking with Tommi. I didn't hear you."

"Well, we're soaked, and you're on my time now—so how about you do your job, and pay me and our clients the respect they deserve. You have plenty of time to flirt with your little girlfriend *after work.*"

Mark nodded, wearily, then helped Mr. Coleman wheel the stretcher through the door and into the elevator. They went down to the basement, into the embalming room, and hoisted the body onto a metal table. Mark did much of the heavy lifting, as Mr. Coleman was a feeble man in the latter half of his sixties.

"Listen. Now I know you're not going to like this, but you've got to get this done tonight," said Mr. Coleman.

"But, Ron, Tommi and I were planning on going out to dinner. Can't we just stick him in the cooler overnight? I'll take care of him first thing in the morning."

"Nope. You've got to get this guy cleaned, pumped, and enhanced by tomorrow evening, for the viewing—and don't forget, you still have to redo Mr. Akel's facial reconstruction by 11 a.m."

"That fast a turnaround on this new guy?! *Christ.*"

"That's the deadline, and I'm certainly not going to fuck up a job 'cause you want to get your willy wet." Coleman cackled lasciviously, breaking his normally stern demeanor.

"Tommi and I have been seeing each other for six months, sir. Tonight's kind of a big deal for her."

"Good for her; she can celebrate all she wants. She leaves, you stay. Now, get started. I'll be back at 8 a.m.," said Mr. Coleman, as he got back into the elevator, leaving Mark with the body.

Mark looked out the small basement window, which was level with the driveway. He waited for Mr. Coleman's Buick to drive past before buzzing Tommi downstairs.

92

"What's up, Mark?" said Tommi, coming down the creaking staircase.

"That son of a bitch left me with a next-day viewing," said Mark, throwing his hands up. "Dinner's off. I'm going to be here all night. I'm really sorry, babe."

Tommi went over to Mark and began rubbing his shoulders. "Don't worry about it. Guiseppe's isn't going anywhere."

Mark turned around and kissed Tommi lightly. "Thanks, Tommi. I'll make it up to you later this week."

"Mr. Coleman did leave, didn't he?" said Tommi, grinning.

"Yeah."

"Well, how about you make it up to me right now?" She grabbed Mark and pulled him in close for another kiss.

"I've got to get to draining this guy," said Mark, nodding toward the body bag.

"In a minute," said Tommi.

Mark seized the opportunity and lifted Tommi off the polished floor and sat with her on one of the tall chairs.

The couple was pawing at each other, Mark beginning to unbutton Tommi's blouse, when the relative silence of the basement was broken by a slight rustling. Mark lifted his head from Tommi's chest and looked around the room. As far as they knew, they were the only ones in the building, save for the corpses stored in the chiller. They held a shared obsession with the deceased, sure, but neither expected anything otherworldly nor, dare say it, paranormal when they heard that mysterious sound in their morbid workplace.

They continued their tryst, breaking several industry codes of conduct, before another, more obvious sound filled the air. It was a heavy groaning, and it seemed to originate from the body bag.

"Mark, are you messing with me again?" Tommi recalled a few instances where Mark and some of the part-timers had played jokes on her, involving shifting body bags and rumbling caskets.

93

Mark shook his head. "No, no. It's probably just some escaping gas."

Despite their inclination toward the rational, Mark and Tommi were not unfamiliar with sudden sensations of foreboding, of a primal revulsion toward death, while on the job. It wasn't uncommon for either to find themselves alone in one of the funeral home's many rooms and pick up on a discomforting ambience, or sense something not quite right about a corpse as it entered their care, though neither had spoken about these feelings openly.

"It's just rigor mortis constricting cavities. Gas escapes the lungs and sometimes you hear what sounds like a moaning or groaning coming from the body. It's creepy, but it's nothing," he said, despite the curious volume and sustained nature of the sounds. He continued kissing her neck.

Soon, however, both Mark and Tommi were forced to admit to an actual presence among them, when an ethereal, vaporous form arose in the room. Mark pulled away from Tommi and the two sprang from the chair. The shape drifted toward Tommi and swirled around her, as she stood unflinchingly still. They watched as the form then wafted back toward the examining table, momentarily hovering over the body bag before dematerializing.

"What *was* that?" asked Tommi, trembling.

"Or *who*?" Mark walked over to the embalming table and slowly unzipped the body bag, curious who he might find inside. Rather than discovering an elderly client, as was typical, Mark found a man about his own age—gaunt, skin cold and blue. Still, nothing he hadn't seen countless times before. Tommi slowly approached the table to see into the bag for herself, and screamed when she saw the man's pallid face.

"Oh my god, it's Cliff!"

"*Who?*"

"Cliff Slater. My ex-boyfriend, from Lestershire High. We dated for a year. Oh my god, what happened to him?" She stared down at Cliff's face, her mouth agape.

"I don't know. Mr. Coleman didn't say."

"Oh god, it was probably something to do with drugs. He had a real problem. He always told me he'd stop. It was one of the reasons we broke up," she said, her eyes welling with tears.

Mark didn't know what to say. He was still taken aback from the encounter with the ghastly shape. "I'm really sorry, Tommi. You should go home. I'll come over when I'm done. But I really need to get to work, and make sure Cliff is ready for his ceremony tomorrow."

"You're really gonna stay?! What about the ghost?"

"We don't know that it was necessarily a 'ghost,' Tommi—and it doesn't really matter. I have too much to do to worry about, whatever it was." After a passionate, parting embrace, Tommi left, while Mark stayed with Cliff's body.

Ordinarily, Mark enjoyed the quiet, still calm of his job. He didn't have to deal with the headaches of grieving loved ones or hospital staff, as Tommi and Mr. Coleman had to—it was just him and the newly deceased. With Tommi's departure, however, Mark felt uneasy in his isolation. As he went through the motions—checking the arteries, bathing and massaging the body—his normally steady hands shook.

He had already drained the body and was incredibly fatigued—as he had worked straight through into the early hours of the morning—when Mark felt cold respiration on his face. Startled, he dropped a suture needle, and splashed chemicals onto the floor from his mobile prep table. A disembodied cackling then filled the sterile room.

At first, Mark attempted to ignore the phantom outburst, and feigned returning to his task at hand, hoping it was just that, an outburst, some sort of temporary, preternatural release. He was running out of time to complete his work, and still had other, unrelated jobs Mr. Coleman would expect him to attend to that morning. He picked up the needle and continued working on Cliff, securing the tube that would fill the man's arteries and vessels with embalming fluid, when the lifeless body began to speak: "You ever diddle a corpse, Mark?"

Mark jumped back from the table. Cliff's mouth hadn't moved, but it certainly sounded like the voice had come from the corpse. "What *are* y- you?" Mark sputtered.

"Dead, Mark."

Mark's first instinct was to run, to get out of the basement and leave the funeral parlor behind, but he was too curious, having never had more than an inkling that the dead *could* haunt the living. "Am I speaking with Cliff Slater?"

"You're a bright one."

Mark realized that the corpse was mocking him, and it got to him. "Listen, Cliff, as far as I know, I've never met you. What's your problem?" He took a few steps back toward the table, gauging whether the corpse was actually producing sound through its vocal cords.

"You're scared, aren't you?" said Cliff's body.

"I've never run into a talking corpse before, and I've dealt with a number of them over the years."

"I don't know why I'm bothering, really. I'm sure you can't help me."

Mark paused to contemplate the ghost's motivations. "Oh, I get it. You need someone living to help you complete some sort of task, so you can move on?"

The disembodied cackling again filled the room. "Sure, just like in the movies, Mark. Can't believe Tommi is actually giving a guy like you the time of day."

"What do you mean by that, Cliff?"

Cliff didn't respond and was unresponsive to any of Mark's further inquiries for the rest of the morning. Mark wanted to stuff Cliff's body back into the chiller and let some other local embalmer finish the job, but he knew it'd be impossible to find someone under such short notice, and he really didn't want to upset Mr. Coleman.

96

Tommi came in extra early, to check up on her boyfriend. She brought him a tall cup of his favorite coffee, from the Bluebird Diner, a breakfast place they frequented, just blocks away from the funeral home.

"So, how'd it go?" asked Tommi, after finding a weary Mark in the office.

"He's done. Can't say it was easy."

"Good job, Mark," said Tommi, who was now rubbing his shoulders. "Coleman's going to owe you big-time after this."

"Hope so." He stood up and examined himself in the wide, antique mirror which hung over a buffet table that they used on the rare occasion that they had a catered event on the premises. "I look like hell."

"You've been up for over 24 hours. I don't see why he wouldn't let you leave early today."

Mark didn't immediately respond, taking his time sipping his coffee in front of the mirror, studying Tommi. "I- uh- I'm not sure if I shouldn't just keep this to myself—but Cliff, er, Cliff's body, it spoke to me last night."

Tommi stepped into view in the mirror's reflection, over Mark's shoulder, her eyes wide. "What do you *mean*? What'd he say?"

"At first it seemed like he was just messing with me. But then he said something like I couldn't help him, and he didn't really respond after that."

"Like he appeared all smoky again?" asked Tommi. "What do you mean by 'messing' with you?"

"No, I didn't see anything, he just sort of talked to me— and it seemed like it was coming from his body. He was pretty rude, for the most part."

Tommi furrowed her brow. "Why would Cliff be rude to you?"

Mark chuckled. "He was kind of a dick, actually."

Tommi's face reddened. "C'mon, Mark, it's not good to speak ill of the dead. And I doubt you'd be in a great mood if you'd just died."

Before they could work out what Mark's encounter might mean, Mr. Coleman barged into the office. "Is it finished? Are we going to be ready for tonight?" He barked orders at his two full-time employees, as they had a funeral that morning, and an additional viewing to get through before Cliff's wake.

"It was a real pain trying to stay awake, but the client's good to go," said Mark, groggily.

Mr. Coleman paid no attention to Mark's subtle complaint. All he said was "Good. Remember, use a little less wax when you redo Mr. Akel this morning, alright?" before exiting the office.

"Asshole," said Tommi, rolling her eyes as their boss left the room. "Anyway, this Cliff thing. I probably should have mentioned it to you last night, but I didn't think it was worth it. It was so long ago, you know? Our relationship was over before I even graduated high school. I just want you to know he doesn't mean anything to me. Okay?"

"Sure, babe," said Mark, wondering why she felt the need to clarify her status with a man who was now deceased.

The couple embraced and began their workdays, Tommi making arrangements for the day's lineup of wakes and funerals, and Mark returning to the basement, to again take on Mr. Akel's final expression.

By mid-morning, Mark desperately needed some caffeine to keep from nodding off. He was making progress readjusting Mr. Akel's chin dimensions and skin tone, and felt he had plenty of time for a break. When Mark headed up to the office, he heard Tommi chatting with someone. Unsure if she was on the phone or with a client, he peeked into the room before entering.

"Wow, really? I can't believe you're gone. I've thought about you, too, over the years."

Mark saw Tommi standing on the other side of the room, in front of the mirror, but couldn't quite hear the reply, or see who she was talking to. He stepped into the room, and caught a glimpse of Cliff's specter reflected in the antique mirror before it quickly vanished. Startled, Tommi looked over her shoulder and spotted Mark standing in the doorway.

"Oh, it's just you," said Tommi. "I'm glad it wasn't Mr. Coleman. He'd probably have a heart attack."

"Would that be such a bad thing?" mumbled Mark. "What were you and Cliff talking about?"

"You saw him?! Yeah, it's really strange; he kind of just appeared in the mirror for a chat." Tommi seemed nearly giddy to Mark.

"What's he want?"

"He does need our help," said Tommi. "He thinks if we can get his mom's engagement ring back from this guy, Justin Smalls, he'll have a chance at passing on."

Mark cringed at the name. "Christ. I went to school with that guy. Last I heard he's a serious dealer."

"Good! If you know him, this might be easier than I thought."

Mark shook his head. "Huh? Why do *we* have to help this guy out? From everything I know about him, he sounds like a real dick. I imagine he gave Smalls his mom's engagement ring in exchange for drugs..."

Tommi understood her fiancé's doubts. "I was sixteen when I met Cliff. He was my first love, you know? He was a 'cool guy' and I fell for him. I really did love him. But I was too naive to see all the red flags. I remember I was working the window at Scoop's Ice Cream—it was my first summer job—when my friend stopped by to tell me she'd seen Cliff making out with this girl at some party. That was just the tip of the iceberg really, because I found out he was cheating on me with multiple girls the whole time we were dating. I didn't believe the rumors, because I never caught him doing anything, or saw him doing drugs. I didn't have the guts to break up with him. If you can believe it, he actually dumped *me* at the end of senior year, after a year and a half of dating!"

Mark grimaced. "You really dealt with that shit for that long? 'Naive' is putting it lightly, Tom."

Tommi scoffed at him. "I was young, *jerk*. Like you never did anything stupid in high school. And he really was a sweet guy when we were together."

Mark knew he had touched a raw nerve and backed off. "Sorry..."

Tommi continued: "So, Cliff didn't treat me right, and I'm glad we broke up, because I learned what I wouldn't accept in a relationship—and it meant I got to meet a guy like you. I know I can be the bigger person, Mark, and I feel like it's my duty to help him out, especially if it's keeping him from resting in peace."

"You want me to find Smalls and get you the ring?" asked Mark, flatly.

"You don't have to be involved at all, Mark. I'm just doing what I think is right."

"I have a buddy whom I'm pretty sure can get me Smalls' number or address. It's no big deal."

Tommi jumped into Mark's arms and kissed his cheek. "Thanks, Marky!"

The rest of the day went off without a hitch for Mark. The Akel family was happy with their grandfather's burial face, and Cliff's family and friends came through and saw off a troubled young man, which afforded Mark the chance to get Justin Small's address from a mutual friend. Mark had even managed to catch a few hours of sleep in between, while Mr. Coleman was off seeing to an afternoon funeral and burial.

Mark and Tommi drove across town that evening, hoping to find Smalls and make a deal with him regarding the ring. "Cliff's mom looked terrible. I can't believe he did that to her," said Tommi.

"Sounded like it was heroin," stated Mark. "Seems like it's always heroin or opiates now."

They pulled into the back of a run-down apartment complex in Binghampton's North Side. Various unsavory characters watched from the back porch as Tommi and Mark left the car and entered the building.

100

"We probably should have called first," said Tommi, examining the seedy interior.

"I got his address, but not his number."

They went up to the third floor and knocked on the door of apartment 3G. The door opened, and a swarthy man appeared. The apartment reeked of marijuana.

"Who are you?" said Smalls. He looked Tommi up and down and grinned.

"Hey, Justin. It's me, Mark Morton. From school. You remember me?"

Justin nodded. "Okay. Come in."

He led them through the ramshackle living space, past an aggressive German Shepherd, and had them sit on a torn-up leather couch.

"What are you looking for?"

"A ring," said Mark.

Smalls started to laugh. "I don't know who sent you here, but this ain't no pawn shop, Morton. Yeah, I remember you."

Tommi looked at Mark nervously.

"Justin, we're just looking to buy back the ring that Cliff Slater gave you," continued Mark.

"Buddy, this really isn't a pawn shop. So, what can I really get you?" Justin reached beneath the coffee table and pulled out a joint, offering it to Tommi.

Tommi declined. Justin shrugged, stuck the joint in his mouth and lit it.

"We heard you had Cliff's mom's engagement ring and we just wanted to buy it back from you, to give it to her as a favor."

Justin stood up without speaking and stretched, revealing a pistol in his belt. Tommi nearly gasped and dug her nails into Mark's arm. Justin then reached into his pocket and pulled out a small bag and tossed it on the coffee table. The bag was filled with a white, powdery substance. "80 bucks."

101

Mark nervously reached into his pocket and pulled out his wallet, handing eighty dollars to Justin for the unwanted substance.

"You sure you don't want a puff?" said Justin to Tommi, as the couple stood to leave.

"No thanks. We've gotta get going," said Tommi, as Mark stuffed the drugs into his pocket.

"See ya around," said Justin, as Mark and Tommi quickly exited the apartment.

Mark hammered the gas pedal, and both breathed a sigh of relief as they left the sketchier part of town.

"I can't believe you just bought drugs. What is it, coke?" said Tommi.

Mark was sweating profusely. "I can't believe it either. I think it's heroin."

"We've got to get rid of it."

"We can't just throw it out the window. And I'm not taking it home."

"And he had a gun!" exclaimed Tommi.

Mark abruptly pulled over and got out with the car still running. "I'll just be a minute," he said, disappearing over an embankment. Not a minute later, he returned and got into the car. "I got rid of it."

"Where?"

"I threw it in the culvert for Pennywise the Clown."

The following morning, when Mark and Tommi showed up for work, they revealed their failure to Cliff, who had appeared as soon as Tommi came into the office.

"We're really sorry, but we couldn't get the ring from Justin. He wouldn't even say whether he still had it," said Tommi.

"He probably pawned it already. But thanks for trying, Tommi. I really appreciate it," said Cliff.

"Isn't this kind of important, Cliff? Like, are you going to wander the Earth for the rest of eternity unless you do whatever it is you're supposed to do?" asked Mark, incredulously.

Tommi glared at her boyfriend. "Mark, be a little understanding here."

"Sure, bro. I'll figure it out," replied Cliff, nonchalantly.

"But your funeral is today. Hmm, maybe it's not like a firm deadline. We can visit a few pawn shops around town this weekend, if we know what we're looking for," said Tommi.

"You've already done enough, Tommi. It's really not your burden," replied Cliff.

"It's like this guy doesn't even give a shit. Even after fucking up his life, he's cool with hanging around in purgatory or whatever," said Mark, angrily.

"Mark, you're being a real jerk. I think there's a body waiting for you downstairs," said Tommi.

Mark threw up his hands and left the room. A new body had just arrived from Floral Nursing and Rehabilitation Center, so he got to work downstairs, draining the blood from the elderly woman. He worked diligently, trying to keep his mind occupied, pleased that this 91-year-old's ghost wasn't harassing him through the embalming process.

Around mid-afternoon, Mark carted the woman to the cooler and went upstairs to grab lunch. As he walked toward the office, he heard talking in an adjacent room. When he looked into the viewing room, he spotted Tommi standing before the vaporous ghost of Cliff Slater, giggling.

"That was a fun show. Remember how drunk Bryan got?" said Tommi to the ghost.

"We had to hold him up through most of Lanemeyer's set," said Cliff, in a throaty, nearly croaking voice.

Tommi laughed. "Good times."

Mark listened in as the one-time lovers recounted more high school memories. When he'd had enough, he returned to the basement, fuming, to finish Mrs. Ward's procedure. He waited until their workday was over before confronting Tommi.

103

"Where have you been all day, Mark?" said Tommi, smiling.

"Working," he replied. "What have you been doing, besides flirting with your dead ex?"

"What?" said Tommi, caught off guard, her cheeks flushed.

"You and Cliff. I heard you guys earlier. Sounded like you were having a good time reminiscing."

"It's not like that. I can't believe you're getting jealous over a dead guy," said Tommi. "I thought you were one of the good ones, Mark. Guess not." She grabbed her purse and left.

When Mark returned to the funeral home the next day, Tommi wouldn't speak to him, so he went down to the basement and got to work. Not long after, he began feeling remorseful for not being more understanding of Tommi's predicament. He couldn't imagine being haunted by the ghost of an ex-girlfriend whom he still had feelings for.

Mark made his way back upstairs to the office, intent on apologizing. But when he opened the door, his worst fears were realized: Tommi was passionately kissing a fully manifested Cliff Slater.

"What the *hell* is going on here?!" said Mark, aghast.

Tommi pulled away from the ghost, suddenly unsure herself of what she was doing.

"It was meant to be, Mark," said Cliff. "My one regret in life was losing Tommi, and somehow, for some reason, we've got a second chance."

Mark laughed nervously. "Can you believe this clown?" he said, looking for Tommi to acknowledge the absurdity of the situation. But she said nothing, as if she were mesmerized.

"Mark, it's over," said Cliff. "Why I'm here, what I was meant to do, was look out for Tommi. She was my one true love. I'm going to be by her side for the rest of her life and beyond. This is bigger than your fleeting mortal fling."

104

Mark rolled his eyes and laughed louder. "Listen to this guy, Tommi. He's delusional. You think he's going to be there for you in death when he couldn't show up for anything, or anyone, in life?"

"I'm sorry, Mark, but I still love him," said Tommi, with little emotion.

"Six months and you're going to leave me for a ghost?" Mark laughed. "I can't even believe I'm saying this."

"I'm sorry, Mark…"

Mark stormed out of the building, pushing past an incensed Mr. Coleman, unable to comprehend Tommi's actions or how easily she could push him aside.

At the cemetery that afternoon, Tommi and Cliff watched Cliff's burial services from a distance. A small group of family and friends were gathered, listening as a priest said the final prayers over the coffin.

After the service, when most of the crowd had dispersed, Tommi was surprised to see Mark appear and approach Cliff's mother. They talked briefly, before Mark handed her something. Upon accepting the item, Cliff's mother smiled and gave Mark a hug.

Curious, Tommi came close enough to hear the tail end of the conversation.

"I was about to throw out the clothes that Cliff arrived in, when I felt something in the pocket. I figured you were the person to give it to."

"I don't know how to thank you. I was sure that he had sold it. It was my engagement ring and has been in my family for generations. So, thank you, Mark."

Mark turned and walked toward Tommi, making eye contact with her, as Cliff took form beside her.

"Where'd you get the ring?" asked Tommi, flatly.

"I had a productive conversation with Justin Smalls," replied Mark.

"Why would you go out of your way to do that?"

105

Before Mark could answer, the sky and cemetery darkened. The wind picked up, whipping Tommi's long, blond hair across her face. They watched as garish, nebulous forms emerged from Cliff's grave and drifted toward Cliff and Tommi. Cliff seemed to understand who they were coming for and tried to flee, but was quickly surrounded and enveloped by the ghastly, black shapes. Tommi screamed as Cliff was dragged down to his grave, to his final resting place.

The clouds parted, and the cemetery was again awash in sunlight. Cliff's mother looked over strangely at Tommi.

"Why would you do that? Did you know what would happen? Where did they take him?" Tommi shouted at Mark.

"I did it for you, Tommi. It was like he had you under some sort of spell."

Tommi would have hit Mark then, believing that his motivation was simply to drive a wedge between her and Cliff, but she saw that Mrs. Slater was still watching. When she paused and really looked at the woman's placid expression, however, Tommi understood then that Mark had done more for Cliff's mother than Cliff ever had. He had given her some semblance of peace after a lifetime of torment.

"I- I'm sorry, Mark. I don't know what came over me," said Tommi. "I love you and I'm ashamed I let such an asshole as Cliff back into my life."

Mark held Tommi's hand and cracked a smile. "It wasn't easy getting that ring back..."

Tommi grinned and embraced him. That evening they finally had their six-month anniversary dinner at Giuseppe's Italian Restaurant.

Play it Again, Sam

The idea had been stewing in Sam Mallory's mind for months—to get a glimpse not only into the past, but *his* past, the one where he and his ex-wife, Melissa, were still together. As one of dozens of engineers working on CRONOS, a fully immersive, intelligent, virtual-reality technology, he couldn't help but think about it. R.M. Snüd Labs wanted to use its groundbreaking technology to offer consumers virtual tours, and more remarkably, to allow its users to experience historical events in "real-time," from a first-person perspective.

Any major event caught on camera—the JFK assassination, Woodstock, the fall of the Berlin Wall—could be fed into their next-gen quantum computer, which would then render, using its burgeoning AI, a full-3D landscape to explore, and computer-generated composite characters with whom to interact. And not only was it meant to be a visual experience, but a tactile one as well. Sam and his team had made a breakthrough into isocortical interfaces, and were progressing toward a virtual experience which could transmit nearly every aspect of touch to the user, without having to rely on smart-garments.

However, Sam was growing impatient with management, and with his counterparts in the Visual Simulation Department. Snüd was still years from a market-ready product, and Sam felt that the company was too risk-averse in testing the technology. The only environment in which he and his team were allowed to test their tactile stimulation interface was a simple, 3D-rendered warehouse. They had mastered the manipulation of simple polygonal objects within months. Then they designed new, more complicated objects, like chairs and beds. They played catch with a virtual football and actually felt the impact on their hands, and even against their chests and stomachs, as they trapped the ball.

All that work, and so little to show for it, thought Sam. He and his team believed that the tech they had developed was ready for the myriad inputs that would accompany immersion in a crowd, the rush of parachuting or jumping off a cliff. But management was hesitant to test the isocortical interfaces in an environment that might overstimulate the brain or, worse-case scenario, lead to brain damage or even death.

Sam's answer to their risk assessment was beyond unorthodox. He was an experienced proponent of experimentation with N,N-Dimethyltryptamine (DMT), and believed that a controlled DMT trip would actually mitigate the overstimulation brought on by an event like, say, a World Series game at Yankee Stadium. Many of Sam's theories on the project were laughed at behind his back by upper management, and he was routinely told to not overextend himself. Higher-ups often implied to Sam that if he wished to continue working on pioneering technologies, he would need to learn how to curb his unorthodox methods.

Sam's long hours at Snüd had certainly strained his relationships. In fact, his dedication to his work was one of the leading factors in his divorce. He and Melissa held joint custody of their four-year-old son, Sebastian, and saw each other once a week. Sam longed to see his family reunited, even a year after the divorce had been finalized.

But to Sam's friends and family, it appeared as though he *had* moved on from his failed marriage. For seven months, he had been in a relationship with an attractive, grounded woman named Sadie. Together they lived in an expensive home in the hills of Lestershire, NY. They had a cat named Zinger, which they both adored, and had even talked of the possibility of marriage and children. Sadie had been understanding, at first, and rarely voiced her concerns regarding Sam's time at work, or his penchant for regularly rewatching old holiday and vacation videos of his old life with Melissa and Sebastian. In actuality, Sam hadn't moved on, wasn't ready for true intimacy, and was far from letting go of his past.

One evening, Sadie finally confronted Sam about his emotional distance from her (and his physical distance too, as he was always at the office). He was in his basement office, in front of his laptop, scrolling through old Facebook photos. Sam responded in a way that told her he was indifferent—and indifference wasn't something she was willing to accept.

"Sam, I'm going to need more from you, if we're going to make this work long-term. It seems like lately all you do is go to work, come home, and go on your computer and do who knows what. I'm only *thirty*. I want to go out with my boyfriend and have fun. I want us to actually be *together* when we're at home together—for at least a few hours, anyway. You have to give me something to work with. The way things are going right now isn't working for me."

"My hours are the same as they've always been, Sadie," said Sam, one eye still on his laptop screen. "I don't get where this animosity is coming from. It's so unlike you."

Sadie leaned over his shoulder to see his computer. "You're literally down here looking at pictures and videos of you and your ex-wife from ten years ago!" Her cheeks had reddened. "Why are we together? If you're just waiting on her to figure it out—I certainly don't want to be around. She treated you like dirt! What do I have to do to get your *full* attention?!"

Sam grabbed her hand to console her, but she yanked it away. "Melissa isn't a part of my life anymore. Sebastian and you have my full attention. I hear what you're saying, Sadie. I love you and I'll make more time for you and me."

Sadie wasn't having it. She was used to Sam saying all the right things, but never following through. "I hope so, Sam. I *do* love you. I know we could have something great together, if you'd quit trying to sabotage it."

"We'll work it out. Marriage and kids, and decades of great things. It's going to be amazing, it's going to be beautiful!" said Sam, mimicking Donald Trump.

Sadie cracked a smile. "Okay, Mr. President. But I'll be watching."

Sam told her to head upstairs and find a movie for them to watch together with Sebastian. He was supposed to pick up his son after Melissa got off work. Once Sadie left, Sam opened a video, which he had minimized when she came down, from the beach vacation he had taken to Aruba with a then five-months-pregnant Melissa.

"This is the one," Sam said to himself, softly. He was about to follow through with an experiment he had been planning for months, a journey into the unknown where mind meets machine.

Sam had never transcended the material world (leaving behind the body to explore other dimensions), nor had he interacted with angels or otherworldly beings, as many proponents of DMT, "the Spirit Molecule," claimed was possible. That stuff, he knew, was nonsense. But in his dozens of DMT trips over the years, he *had* felt an awareness like no other, a sense of reality that was more distinct, more detailed than the reality of his everyday. On DMT he experienced an unparalleled catharsis, a rush of emotion, in each of his explorations, and now he wanted to relive his past with the sensory advantages that the drug offered.

It was for this reason that he had brought with him to the basement a moderate dose of DMT. The CRONOS unit sat on his desk, beside his laptop. He had taken it from the secured cold room at work only hours prior. (It being a Friday in July, most everyone had gone home after lunch.) He plugged a makeshift helmet and visor into the unit, which he had painstakingly tested at work during his breaks. The helmet utilized his team's isocortical interface. The most difficult task was getting the visor to communicate with the iso interface without lag. It had taken months to get to that point.

Sam sat at his desk and put on the helmet. From his pocket, he removed a small thumb drive containing the software he had developed for his experiment, which he plugged into the unit, writing over its standard programming. No one in his office would have ever approved, but Sam thought that accessing personal videos would aid in a more fruitful, and immersive, experience. He believed that the brain would be better equipped to interpret actual memories, which was the main reason why he had chosen a series of videos he was acutely familiar with.

Sam connected CRONOS to his laptop, queued his personal video library, and sent the first of the videos to the unit's drive. He then injected himself with the DMT, before powering on CRONOS and placing the visor over the top half of his face. He relaxed back into his leather chair and stared into the blank screen of the visor, waiting for the program to begin, and for the DMT to take hold.

Suddenly, the artificial lighting of his basement was replaced by the lively warmth of the Caribbean sun. And more amazing than the sensation of the sunlight was the soft, hot sand beneath his feet. He heard the splashing of water, children laughing—and the voice of Melissa, telling him how much she was enjoying the book she held in her hands. Melissa's most prominent feature at the time was her stomach. She was five months into her pregnancy with Sebastian, and the bump stuck out from her slender frame.

"Sam, would you mind grabbing me another water?" she asked. Sam shivered and felt comforted by the sound of her voice. It had worked! He had broken protocol, but he had done it! He was fully immersed in a 3D-rendered model; he could *feel* the artificial environment and was interacting with a computer-generated character. Forget about virtual football.

"Sure thing, honey," he said. He lifted the lid of the cooler and felt the hard plastic against his fingers. He stuck his hand inside the chill container, removed a plastic water bottle, and handed it to Melissa. The moment wasn't overly romantic or particularly memorable, but it was still pleasantly nostalgic, and that was enough for Sam.

"I'd get up, but, you know," said Melissa, smiling and looking down at her bulbous belly.

Sam snickered. "Oh, that—" He paused mid-sentence, realizing that he was about to say something that would set her off and send them back to their hotel room not ten minutes later.

"*What?*" asked Melissa.

"I'm just glad you decided to wear the bikini, instead of that one-piece suit you had picked out. You look absolutely stunning, Mel," said Sam. He then considered the insensitivity of his original statement: "Oh, that beach ball is holding you down?" In the video, as it had originally played out, Melissa grew quiet, then threw a fit over his little jab at her pregnant stomach. Not portrayed in the video was how, after returning home, days later, Melissa revealed to Sam that his comment had upset her greatly, and had practically ruined their last vacation together before the arrival of Sebastian.

The video continued for a few more minutes, as he and Melissa sunned on the beach, discussing their future, names for the baby, and the seafood restaurant where they wanted to dine that evening. Every shared smile with Melissa, every flutter of her eyelashes, seemed as authentic as if she were more than a computer-generated creation. Flesh and blood.

Without warning, Sam was pulled from the simulation and fully cognizant of his place in the basement; the sound of the rushing waves and the warmth on his skin again nothing more than a memory captured. He removed the visor, still somewhat light-headed due to the DMT. As he powered down the unit and his laptop, he felt wistful, and slightly perplexed. He had altered the events of the video in a way he

112

couldn't have imagined, and he delighted in being able to do so. The experience had a more pleasing outcome than the video itself, which hindsight had provided him: a few more calm moments with Melissa, as they were when they were fully invested in one another. If only it had been real, he thought.

Sam's experience with the CRONOS unit was still in his thoughts as he rang the doorbell at Melissa's house, to pick up Sebastian. He cherished the evenings he had with his son, but Sam always felt uncomfortable during the brief exchanges with Melissa. She was still as stunning as in those days in Aruba, yet she might as well have been on the other side of the planet. She rarely bothered looking him in the eye when they met. Melissa had moved on—she had dated several men since their divorce, and was usually curt and snarky when she and Sam interacted.

The door opened. Sebastian stood three-feet-tall by his mother's side, wearing his favorite Spider-Man backpack.

"Hey, buddy!" said Sam, smiling.

"Hi, Daddy," said Sebastian, wearing his father's smile.

"How are ya, Sam?" asked Melissa.

"I'm great," he replied. "Busy at work, as usual. You?"

"We're short-staffed this week, so it's been a little hectic," said Melissa, who worked as an accountant at Farrell Dench. "I could use a vacation, to be honest."

"I hear you." Sam thought about his virtual replay of their beach vacation. "Hey, speaking of which—remember that trip to Aruba before Sebastian was born? It popped up as one of my Facebook Memories the other night."

Melissa smiled. "How could I forget? It was a dream vacation... What about it?"

"It *was?*" Sam had discussed the trip with her in subsequent years. They often dissected it during long arguments, when they were having trouble adjusting to their new life as parents. She regularly used it as an example of

113

how they fell short as a couple, where he had failed to live up to her expectations of a loving, supportive husband.

"Yeah. I'd like to go there again sometime. I wonder if that seafood place still exists? What was it—The Lobster House, er, Cabana? That calamari was to *die* for."

Sam took a moment to reply, as he was perplexed by Melissa's statement about the trip being a great memory for her. The Lobster Cabana had been discussed, but after his "beach ball" comment, they had decided to stay in and order room service—they never went out to eat that night. "What do you mean? We didn't eat at the Lobster Cabana."

"Your memory is terrible. Yes, we did. We tanned on the beach for a few hours, then we went to The Lobster Cabana. We had this exceptional fried calamari with marinara for an appetizer."

Sam stood, dumbfounded, while Sebastian began to yank at his hand. Sam had rewatched the video countless times over the years, likely hundreds of times in the throes of depression, and now she was passing over what had always been the most crucial detail for her, as if it had never happened: his nasty remark about her gravid belly. "If you say so," said Sam, trying to make sense of it. "Well, I'll bring him back around nine."

Having Sebastian around was simultaneously comforting and a source of stress for Sam. He loved his son, but Sam couldn't look into the child's eyes without thinking of Melissa and the life he had lost. Still, Sam always managed to squeeze in some quality time with the boy between his work obligations and Melissa's schedule. That evening, he and Sadie took Sebastian out to Plucky's Pizza Place.

Sebastian was playing in the arcade while Sam and Sadie stood nearby. They attempted to carry on a conversation amid the cacophony of noise produced by screaming kids and arcade cabinets.

"You've got a cute kid, Sam," said Sadie, smiling as Sebastian excitedly cranked the steering wheel of a racing game.

"He's alright," replied Sam, grinning. "Needs to work on his shifting, though."

"True." Sadie's smile quickly faded. "It's nice getting out of the house for once."

"Yeah."

"Listen, I know you're busy with work stuff, but it'd be nice for *us*—just me and you—to go out, at least once a week. Spend more time together, you know?"

Sam was quiet.

"Sam…"

"I heard you. And I'll say what I said before: I'm passionate about my work, and I'll make time for us."

Sadie didn't reply. She spent the remainder of their night skulking, Sam doing what he could to enjoy the time out with Sebastian.

Late that night, Sam snuck out of bed and stole down to the basement for another demo of the CRONOS. His initial run had proven exceptionally realistic, and he was excited to explore more simulations with that same level of authenticity.

He injected DMT, put on the visor, and loaded up another old video.

The transition was instantaneous. There he was, in Melissa's house—his former home—on Christmas morning. He sat on the floor of the living room, feeling the fibers of the grey (it was the exact shade of grey) rug on his fingers. The room smelled of Christmas-scented candles and gingerbread, and Paul McCartney's "Wonderful Christmastime" played on the stereo. The effect was so realistic that, for a moment, Sam wondered if he wasn't there, a witness to a Christmas past, like old Ebenezer.

Most importantly, though, and what made the experience magical for Sam, was the presence of Melissa and a 3-month-old Sebastian, who lay within a motorized swing, cooing. He

115

was surprised to see Melissa smiling at him, as his memory was that she had been upset that entire holiday season. Then he saw the gift bag in her hands and knew what was about to come.

She yanked the red tissue paper from the bag and looked inside—and there was the frown that Sam remembered. Melissa looked like a petulant child about to erupt.

"What's this?" she asked, lifting a large, purple purse out of the bag. It was leather, with gold straps.

"The lady at the Forget-Me-Not Shoppe said this was one of their top sellers," said Sam, finding himself repeating the same lines that he had originally spoken. "You don't like it?"

Melissa pouted over the gift, saying how she expected something more meaningful, considering how this was their first Christmas with Sebastian and in their new home.

Sam felt the same frustration he had felt years before. He had originally called her out, saying, "How do you not know how to receive a *gift* as an adult? You practically stomp your feet like my spoiled niece when you receive something you're not fond of." But he knew better; he knew how she would react, and it wasn't pretty. Then a thought came to him. Melissa would later use the purse as a makeshift baby bag, and it would become a memento for her, of her early years with Sebastian.

"Honey, I'm sorry you don't like the purse. I went to a bunch of stores to find something I thought you'd really like. I mean it. I'll return it, if you don't want it." Sam couldn't help but cringe at his showing of servility, but he continued: "Listen, maybe you could use it as a baby bag? What do you think about that? It's a pretty big purse, and I'm sure you could fit a decent amount of diapers and wipes in there. Maybe some snacks and a few toys, too. It'd be the most stylish baby bag around!"

In the red-and-white glow of the tree, Melissa smiled. She looked at the bag, then back at Sam. "You know, it *could*

116

make a good baby bag. A weird one—I don't think I've seen any purple leather baby bags before—but it might work…. I'm sorry for getting upset. Thanks for the gift, Sam."

"You're welcome, honey," replied Sam, amazed at how easy it was to manipulate a formerly dour situation, due to having replayed it so many times.

Melissa leaned over and planted a kiss on his cheek. "Now, how about breakfast?"

The simulation ended with Melissa picking up Sebastian, and Sam was back in the basement—that Christmas morning again nothing more than a memory.

Sam was still elated by his brief—altered—encounter with Melissa when his phone rang that Saturday afternoon. It was her.

"Hi Sam."

"Hi Melissa." He felt a closeness to her then that he hadn't felt in ages. "What's up?"

They proceeded to discuss Sebastian for a considerable chunk of time—his school, friends, fascination with airplanes—before Melissa turned the conversation inward.

"To be honest, Sam, I've been thinking about you…umm…wondering how you've been. How *are* you? Is the job going well?"

Sam couldn't believe what he was hearing. He and Melissa had not spoken about anything other than Sebastian since their divorce, apart from legalities. That she was expressing some interest in *his* life perplexed him. What was going on? After both of his CRONOS experiments, he had really seen a change in Melissa's attitude toward him. Wild ideas began to form in his mind. Could it be more than a simulation? Was the DMT allowing him some sort of manipulation over reality—the past, even? He needed to further test his theory that Melissa's view of him had indeed improved.

"So, I'll have Sam in the morning on Thanksgiving, right? Then bring him over?"

117

"Yes, that's the plan," replied Melissa.

"I hope he has a nice holiday. I'm a terrible cook; I burned the turkey last year. I guess holidays just aren't my thing…." He cringed at his roundabout way of getting to his point. "*Ha*, remember Sebastian's first Christmas? *Ouch.*"

"What are you talking about?" Melissa giggled. "That was a *wonderful* Christmas. I still use that bag when I take him to karate, ya know!"

Sam paused. *Holy shit! It's real!* What had once been a fantasy, something he had only explored in the worst days of his depression, was now a reality: to relive and, more importantly, alter his past.

"You there?" asked Melissa, after Sam didn't respond.

"Yes, yes, I'm here. That's fantastic you still use the bag. *Haha.* Hey, it's really nice to talk to you, Mel."

"You haven't called me *that* in a while," she said, softly.

Sam chuckled. "I guess not. So, I was thinking it might be nice if we both took Sebastian to the zoo…" He knew it was a risky thing to ask, that he was pushing his luck and would still likely get rejected.

"Hmm. We haven't done anything together in such a long time… But it would be good for Sebastian to see that we can stand each other for more than a couple minutes at a time." Melissa sighed. "Sure, I'll go."

They talked for another half hour, Sam giddy at the prospect of rekindling their relationship.

"I'll see you Tuesday," said Melissa. "Sebastian's going to have so much fun. Me too, I think."

"Yep. Hey, it was really nice talking—" Sam stopped at the sound of the front door opening. It was Sadie. "Talking to you."

Sam quickly said goodbye and put down the phone before Sadie walked into the room. He didn't waste any time. As soon as he had greeted Sadie, and she had gone upstairs to shower, he went back down to the basement and fired up the CRONOS unit. This time Sam had a very specific goal in

118

mind. He only had a few videos to work with, but this one was pivotal. DMT injected, visor on, video loaded. *Go.*

The transition from reality to the simulation was more jarring than on his previous attempts, and Sam had to take a moment to adjust to the sensory overload. Bright, colorful balloons. The scents of vanilla frosting and pizza. The chatter and squeals of young children as they ran through the party room of Manic Monkeys, the family entertainment center where Sebastian's third birthday party had been hosted. His son was opening presents in a corner of the room, to the cheers of his young friends and their parents. Unlike the other videos Sam had accessed, this one was more recent; it had been shot just months before he and Melissa separated. There she stood—the recreation was uncanny—cleaning up paper plates covered in cake and ice cream, half-empty cups of Hawaiian Punch. To say Melisa looked perturbed, displeased, would be an understatement. She and Sam had argued violently in the car on the way there, which had become quite the norm by that point in their relationship.

The simulation started, as Sam remembered, with him standing across the room, avoiding his then-wife. He knew that this moment was crucial. This time around, he wouldn't just sit there—arms crossed, moping. This time he did what he should have done then, had he not been so prideful, and walked up to Melissa. She didn't look up. She had acted as if he wasn't there from the moment they'd arrived.

"Melissa…"

"What do you want, Sam? Why are you filming me?"

"Let me help."

"I don't need your help," she said, tossing paper plates into an open garbage bag.

"Mel, I'm sorry for being a dick. Go sit down with Sebastian. Enjoy yourself. I'll take care of this mess. You threw a good party. You're a great mom. Everyone's having a lot of fun."

Melissa stopped what she was doing and gave Sam her full attention. "Really?"

"Yeah. I should be doing my part. And I should be helping more at home, too."

Melissa smiled faintly. She began to walk over to Sebastian, but stopped and gave Sam a kiss on the cheek. "Thanks, Sam."

Sam felt elated, and speculated about what might be the new outcome, once he was out of the simulation. He wondered if his actions here could cause some sort of ripple effect and greatly change his present. Maybe when the video ended, and he was back in reality, he and Melissa would still be together—or, at least, closer to it. Maybe this was the moment he needed to finally show Melissa that he was a compassionate, loving partner worthy of her time and attention.

When he was done cleaning the party room, Sam played a few arcade games with Sebastian, while Melissa looked on, smiling. He knew the simulation wouldn't last forever, so he basked in the moment, hoping that what he had done there had really meant something.

But as quickly as he had entered the simulation, he was pulled out of it—but not by his own volition. He knew he still had time on the video. The party scene was gone because the visor had been yanked from his face. Sam was gradually coming to, recalibrating his senses to the sudden shock, and returning to his place in the basement. He wasn't alone. Sadie hovered over him, holding the CRONOS visor in her hand.

"Sam, get up. Your boss is at the door. He wants to talk to you, now. He seems really upset."

Sam was surprised that she didn't seem mad, but fearful. "Okay, okay." Sam pried himself from the chair and stumbled up to the first floor, his head and body aching, still feeling the effects of the DMT and reeling from the abrupt transition. He got to the front door, where his supervisor stood, with three burly men he didn't recognize.

"Collin. What's going on?"

"Where's the unit?" asked Collin, sternly.

Sam tensed. He was well-aware that employees were forbidden from taking any technology home. "Oh, CRONOS? Collin, I know we're not supposed to leave campus with it, but I think I'm really onto something here, man. I wanted to give it my full attention…"

"I don't want to hear any excuses. Goddammit, Sam, you're lucky I didn't call the cops. Where is it?"

"Just, just hold on." Sam went back to the basement and picked up the CRONOS unit. He stood for a moment, staring at it, contemplating its potential and all of the things he could still *change*, before returning it the men at his door.

"Hand it over," said Collin.

"Collin, if you just gave me a little more time. You wouldn't believe what I've accomplished with it…"

"Hand it over or I *will* get the police involved, alright?"

"But Collin—"

"Now!"

Collin took the unit from Sam, and he and his men left without another word. Sam watched his gateway to the past slip out of his hands, likely for good. He knew he would be terminated immediately and could only hope that the company wouldn't press charges.

When he closed the door behind him, Sadie was standing there, waiting, and holding his laptop in her hands.

"Sadie, I can explain…"

"Don't." She lifted the laptop, showing him the playlist he had left open: the Aruba vacation, Christmas Day, Sebastian's birthday party. "What are you doing always watching these videos of your ex-wife? Why did these guys come to our house for that machine? What were you using it for?"

"I… Those aren't just videos of me and Melissa. Sebastian's in them."

"Sam, stop; it's not only videos 'with Sebastian.'"

121

"*Sadie*, there's nothing going on between Melissa and me. What's wrong with watching some old movies from when your kid was a baby?"

Sadie shook her head. "I can't do this anymore. I can't be with a guy who's stuck in the past."

"Sadie…" Sam felt a tinge of regret, but in his heart, he knew Sadie wasn't the one.

"I'm done, Sam," she said, glumly. "I love you, but it's over. I've already asked my sister if I can move in with her. I'll have my stuff out of here this weekend."

Sadie walked away and headed up to the second floor. She wasn't even to the top of the staircase when Sam hurriedly grabbed his car keys and left the house. He needed to see Melissa. To find out if his final simulation had done anything to resuscitate her love for him.

Sam was a ball of emotion as he drove through town. He knew it was late to be visiting unannounced, especially given their history, but he felt an uncontrollable urge to see if there would be any payoff from his latest experiment.

When he pulled up to her house, Sam was surprised to see an unfamiliar silver Jeep in the driveway. Melissa hadn't mentioned buying a new car, and she liked to park in the garage. It was probably a visitor, he thought. He hadn't seen any of her family in some time. Sam parked, and walked up her front steps. He was still nervous when he rang the doorbell.

Only a moment passed before Melissa opened the door. She looked surprised to see Sam, even irritated. "Sam? What's going on? Where were you?"

"I know it's sort of late, but I wanted to talk to you. See I—" Sam stopped when he caught sight of the scene inside. There was a middle-aged man with grey hair in the living room, playing with Sebastian. "Hey, who's that?" asked Sam, pointing inside.

Melissa looked over her shoulder, before replying. "That's Donnie. We've been dating for a few months now."

122

"Oh," said Sam, shocked that she hadn't mentioned the man during any of their recent heartfelt conversations. He was disappointed that his actions at the birthday party hadn't turned the course of things more in his favor. Maybe if he could manage to access the unit again…

"Why are you here, Sam? It's too late. He was real disappointed when you didn't show," said Melissa.

"Huh? Who was disappointed?" He kept staring inside at this new man. Sam had practically been on the verge of professing his undying love to Melissa, but now felt, unexpectedly, unwelcome. "So, are we still going to the zoo this week?"

Melissa cocked her head. "The zoo? *Huh?*"

"You agreed we could take Sebastian to the zoo together. This Tuesday?"

There was a moment of silence before Melissa responded: "I have no idea what you're talking about. I take him to the zoo now and then, but why would we go together, Sam? We can't spend more than ten minutes together without getting into a fight. Besides, I'm seeing Donnie and it doesn't seem right."

"You don't remember our conversation from the other night?"

"No."

"We talked about Aruba. Remember, when you were pregnant, and what a good time we had?"

"*Ha.* A *good time?* You told me my stomach looked like a beach ball, Sam. I'm *still* not over it."

Sam didn't understand. He was certain they had discussed it, the outcome of the new timeline. "What about our phone call from the other day when we talked about Christmas. Remember, Sebastian's first Christmas?"

"Sam, I don't get it. Why are you here trying to mess with me?"

"C'mon, Melissa," said Sam, anxiously. "We talked about your purse."

123

Melissa snickered. "Yeah, I remember. You started a fight and ruined Sebastian's First Christmas. You told me that I was a child and didn't know how to receive a gift! Whatever that means... Are you here to remind me of all the shit you put me through in our marriage?"

"But...that's not how it happened. I changed it..."

"I'm really confused. Are you on something now, Sam?" Melissa leaned in. "Are you *fucking* tripping right now?"

Sam ignored her accusation. "I did the right things. I shut my mouth at the beach. I helped clean up at Sebastian's birthday party. I made things right."

"I don't know what you're getting at, Sam. I wish you had been more present in those moments, and been more thoughtful of me, but you weren't. There's no use apologizing now. It's in the past and there's no reason to dredge it up again. Sebastian and I are happy with how things are now, and if you want to have a relationship with him, you're going to have to actually show up when you say you will."

Sam's lip quivered, his foot tapped nervously on her front stoop. "I felt like we connected over the last couple days. Those long phone calls. You made it seem like things were different."

"What the hell are you talking about? I haven't seen or spoken to you since last Friday. I don't recall any phone conversations. You're being a real creep. I don't have time for this, alright?"

Donnie had come to the door, after hearing how the conversation had become combative.

"Who the *hell* is this old man, anyway?" asked Sam.

"It's none of your business. I'll drop Sebastian off at your house next week," said Melissa, who started to close the door.

"Melissa, wait..."

"Don't bother coming by anymore, Sam," she said, shutting the door.

124

Crestfallen, Sam walked back to his car. In his rush to get over to Melissa's, he hadn't bothered to check his phone. It was then that he saw it was Friday, July 15, the day he had taken the CRONOS unit home. There were messages from Melissa asking him why he wasn't picking up Sebastian, why he was ignoring her calls. A week *hadn't* passed, as he had thought. The phone calls, the pleasant conversations with Melissa, all of it was a creation of his mind. A simulation. He had accomplished something monumental in his DMT-fueled experiments, but it wasn't time travel or any metaphysical manipulation of the real world. With the help of the Spirit Molecule, his mind had filled in the spaces between the videos he had uploaded. It was wish-fulfillment made *near-reality*. He had proven the power and potential of the technology, to the detriment of his career and personal life. CRONOS really could make you feel like you were reliving moments captured on film or video.

As he sat in his car—Melissa gone again, Sadie gone for good, his career all but over—he could only hope that he was still in a simulation, moments from re-entering some sort of tolerable reality.

126

Beyond a Blood Moon

I was awakened one night in bed, likely due to the absence of my fiancée; I can only assume that it was this silence past midnight, which a light sleeper can't help but notice once they've become attuned to the constancy of their nightly bedroom environment. And this absence was likely what my unconscious found unsettling enough to stir me. Sara's breathing was often measured, hypnotic, a comforting rhythm to my night. Her respiration was often the last thing I took hold of in my twilight mind before plunging into the great unknown, and then my first lifeline back to cognizance each morning. But when I stirred that night, due to the silence, and reached for her—I couldn't help but convulse, considering a multitude of fears and possibilities.

I left the bedroom and wandered our home. Her sneakers were gone. She enjoyed jogging late, and I hated that she had no fear of the night. As I dressed and put on my shoes, I considered whether I was the reason for her jogging now; that she wouldn't want to worry me if I were still awake, while she took the path around the block and through the cemetery. So, since there was no way I was going to fall back to sleep without seeing her safely home, I headed out into the night.

There were intermittent clouds, but the moon was full and bright, illuminating the areas where the amber-yellow street lamps fell short. As I turned from the sidewalk and into Valleyview Cemetery, I noticed the beginnings of a lunar eclipse. I hadn't seen one since childhood and stood in awe as the Earth's shadow consumed the reddening lunar surface. At the time, I considered how strange and seemingly unimportant such a spectacular astronomical event had been to me. It had been over twenty years since I'd stood in my parents' front yard and last waited for the moon to vanish.

I rarely consumed local media, but there had to have been some mention of it in the newspaper that morning. To think that ancient societies would plan for months, and even years, in advance, to celebrate a full lunar eclipse—and here I was, casually catching one as I searched for my missing companion.

I continued on through Valleyview after the blood moon had passed. The lunar disc retained some of its reddish hue, but the street lamps on either end of the cemetery were enough for me to find my way down the winding paths of the hillside graveyard. I came upon Sara, not far from the central outcropping of mausoleums. I ran to her crumpled form. I knew her instantly by the powder-blue sneakers with their pink bands.

She was lifeless. I screamed her name as I attempted to revive her. I could make out the strangulation marks on her neck, her bruised face, as I gave my best effort at resuscitation. She had been murdered. I'm still not sure whether she had been robbed. I called 911 and the paramedics, fire department, and police raced into the cemetery.

It was the last time I saw Sara's body, as her family wouldn't allow me at the wake or funeral, since I was awaiting arraignment for homicide.

I had no choice but to put my hands on her and try my best to revive her. I had to touch her, feel with my own hands the bruising on her cheek, her broken right orbital bone, the sinewy strangulation marks on her neck. I began to mourn her, long before the first medic arrived on the scene.

There was no one else to charge, imprison, and punish. It really made sense for the police, community, my friends, and family, that I was the one who had extinguished a loving, generous, woman—one who I had long imagined as the

128

mother of my children, my lifelong partner. For eight years I went mad in a single cell at Shawangunk Correctional Facility. I had no visitors, no one waiting for me—no one to serve my time for. I wrote letters to Sara's family, my own family, pleading my innocence and the truth of my unabashed love for her. They went unanswered.

During my eight years, I married Sara in my mind, had children with her. We went on family vacations, advanced in our careers—even had spats, and differences, which we eventually overcame. She and I advanced into old age, and I was ready to die alongside her when I was granted parole.

The first night I was allowed to leave the halfway house, I went right to Valleyview and lay upon her ornate altar-tomb. It was a frigid, overcast February night, and I intended to fall asleep and become a part of her monument. A monument to my love for her, the love we had shared the four years we were together, and the eight I had shared with her in dream.

With my finger I traced her name in the granite, then the inscription beneath, which read: "Devoted daughter and fiancée, a beautiful soul taken too soon." I shivered at the mention of 'fiancée,' that her parents left her connection to me at her burial site. It surprised me, and gave me some small consolatory pleasure in my waning hours.

The chill had already consumed me and was now leaving my body along with my life's energy. It began to snow. A thin, white blanket covered me and the altar, and I began to drift into that place between conscious and unconscious. But as I resigned myself to my end, and was preparing to embrace my final sleep, the altar moved beneath me. The shock of the tomb cracking mere inches from my face gave me a rush of adrenaline that left me fully cognizant of what then occurred.

From the few inches of darkness revealed by the cracked top piece of the altar, a waxen, partly shriveled hand emerged. I pushed myself onto my side to avoid the ghastly intrusion by my beloved. The aged, embalmed hand proceeded to scratch out the inscription on the tomb. I watched as an eerie

129

incandescent green glow passed from the fingertips to the stone, bright enough that I had to momentarily shield my eyes.

It wasn't half a minute before the task was complete, and the hand returned to the dark of the tomb, the altar gently scraping back to its settled position. I looked to the inscription, to see what damage had been done, but saw nothing out of the ordinary. I assumed I had experienced some sort of delusion brought on by my deteriorating condition.

When I lay back on the tomb, resigned to complete my purpose, I looked up into the overcast sky, and the clouds soon parted—revealing the Earth's colossal umbra as it consumed the moon. I had no prior knowledge of an impending lunar eclipse, and I had to shield my eyes, as I was shaken to my core by the specter of the blood-red disc.

I turned away from the dreadful astronomical event, and when I did, I caught sight of the inscription on the tomb, which was now illuminated in a reddish hue from the heavenly body. Where the inscription had once read "Devoted daughter and fiancée; a beautiful soul taken too soon," it now read, in an ordered (and what I can only describe as 'angelic') script: "Devoted mother and wife; to be together again, if only in dream."

-Preview-

A Made Match

(from the episodic novel *Marvelry's Curiosity Shop*)

Marsha Frampton stared at a pair of wood carvings with large, disc-shaped heads set on an open bookshelf inside Marvelry's Curiosity Shop and called to her husband, Allen. "Honey, check these out."

"What are they?" replied Allen, who was busy admiring a collection of vintage *Weird Tales* magazines.

"I don't know. They look strange, though," said Marsha." Each carving was about eight inches tall. One man, one woman. They were sculpted in a somewhat awkward fashion, with comically exaggerated extremities.

Marsha had her eyes fixed on the male doll (and his disproportionate phallus) when the proprietor's face appeared between the statuettes, grinning at her. She jumped back and squealed, partly in embarrassment.

Dr. Marvelry stood up, laid his hands on top of the bookcase, and leaned forward. He was so close, Marsha got a good whiff of his citrus-scented cologne. "They're African fertility dolls, ma'am. All the way from Ghana."

Marsha eased up. "Fertility dolls?" She looked intrigued.

"Akuaba, handcrafted by the Ashanti people. Well received the world over," said Marvelry, raising his eyebrows in a provocative manner.

Marsha looked over at her husband, who was off in his own world. Seeing he was preoccupied, she turned and whispered to the shopkeeper. "Would these work to improve a man's, umm, stamina?" she asked, blushing slightly.

131

"Perhaps," said Marvelry, a wry smile crossing his face. "Likely more effective than the promise pills and herbal remedies one comes across on late-night TV."

"Well, they're really neat looking. And I wouldn't mind any *added effects*. How much are they?"

Marvelry revealed the price, which caught Allen's attention and prompted him to saunter over.

"That much for two little dolls?" asked Allen, bending down to inspect the carvings. Marsha rolled her eyes at her husband, who would haggle over the price of a candy bar.

"These *dolls* hold immense power, sir. The people of Western Africa have turned to them for centuries as a reliable reproductive aid."

"Oh, I'm sure," said Allen. He looked back at his wife, and he knew *that* look. If he didn't budge, she'd be on him for days. "Okay, how much for just one of 'em?"

"Sir, the woman I bought these from was adamant that they be sold as a pair—as their power comes from their proximity, their union." Marvelry's countenance became suddenly serious, his eyebrows furrowed.

"That's great, but I'm not dropping one-hundred bones on some imported trinkets."

"*Allen,*" said Marsha, looking at her husband sideways.

"We'll take one. The lady," said Allen as he handed his credit card to Marvelry.

At first Marvelry hesitated and considered turning down the man's offer. But ultimately, he wanted to please his customer, so he cheerfully wrapped up the statuette in brown paper and placed it in a plastic bag. "Enjoy. But I make no promises that this doll will have any positive impact on your fecundity, or love life, for that matter. Good day, ma'am. Sir."

The Framptons left and Marvelry spent the next hour doing paperwork and setting up a meeting to sell a 19th-century straight jacket to an up-and-coming magician he knew from a nearby hamlet.

He was just getting off the phone when another couple, Lindsay and Jeff Buckingham, entered the store. Marvelry greeted the thirtysomething pair, who said they were there to purchase a magic set for their son.

"Magic! Why, you couldn't have come to a better place!" said Marvelry.

"So we've heard," said Lindsay, who had been referred to Marvelry by a member of the Binghampton Rotary. "So, what do you suggest for a budding young magician?"

Marvelry led the couple to a shelf lined with wands, hats, scarves, handcuffs, and other staple props. He showed them some of the classics—the torn and restored fifty-dollar bill drew a smile from Lindsay—and put together a solid starter set for their son.

Pleased with their purchase, Jeff and Lindsay followed the shopkeeper to the register. They were about to complete the transaction when Jeff noticed the remaining fertility doll on the shelf. "What's this thing?" he asked, pointing at the small wooden man. "Is this another magic prop?"

"That, sir, is an African fertility doll," said Marvelry as he placed a set of false playing cards into their bag. "Magic of a *different* sort, you might say."

"Is that right?" said Jeff, a mischievous smile crossing his face. He turned to Lindsay. "Honey, that could come in handy, don't you think?" Lindsay shrugged and scowled at her husband.

Jeff turned back to the shopkeeper and said in a low voice, "Let's just say it's been a while."

Without a response—Marverly was a gentleman, after all—the shopkeeper went over to the shelf and removed the doll. He wrapped it up and placed it in the bag. "As a thank-you for purchasing this magic set, I'd like to give this to you as a gift."

Jeff smiled. "Wow, thank you, sir. That's really nice of you."

"We don't need that, Mr. Marvelry, really," said Lindsay, who thought the doll a hideous little thing, and was quite content with her sole child. It really had been a while.

"Honey, c'mon," whispered Jeff to his wife. "It's a nice gesture."

"Whatever," said Lindsay, in a huff, and took the bag from Marvelry. Jeff followed her to the door, but not before turning back to the shopkeeper and slyly grinning.

Marvelry waved goodbye. He was pleased. While the starter set had been expensive, he had mainly given the doll away out of discomfort. He thought the unpaired statuette to be bad luck and wanted it out of his shop as soon as possible.

The first couple that visited Marvelry that day, Marsha and Allen Frampton, had by now returned to their childless home, and placed their new doll on a shelf opposite their bed.

"I love it," said Marsha, standing back a few feet from the shelf, admiring her new purchase. The exotic, dark-brown doll stood in sharp contrast to the bedroom's simple, peach-colored theme.

Allen shook his head. "That thing's weird. And why do we have to have it in the bedroom? Is it going to undo your hysterectomy? Couldn't you put it down in the living room with your other tchotchkes?"

"It's not just supposed to make a woman pregnant, Allen. It's supposed to be an aphrodisiac of some sort for women *and* men. Where else would we put it, on the porch?"

Allen groaned. "You're kidding, right? That doll's gonna give me a stiffy? *Sure.*" He left the room.

The Framptons were lying next to each other in bed that evening—Marsha doing her crosswords and Allen watching baseball on TV—when Marsha felt her husband's hand run up her thigh.

"Allen!" said Marsha, giggling. He hadn't made a move on her in months and she thought he was still upset about the doll.

134

He began to kiss her neck. "Yes, honey?" He continued, adding another hand to the mix.

"Hey, are you sure you're up to it? After what happened *last time?*"

Without saying another word, he took hold of his wife and made sweet, fervent love to her. Marsha was overwhelmed by Allen's sudden endurance; it was like he was twenty again. She closed her eyes and experienced a pleasure she had previously given up the possibility of. The room suddenly felt warmer, stifling almost, as if someone had cranked up the thermostat. Allen's thrusts were so zealously ordered, heartfelt, that she nearly passed out following her peak moment.

Across town, Jeff Buckingham set he and Lindsay's fertility doll on his bedroom dresser, next to a bottle of his favorite cologne. "Look, honey. Maybe this will help with our little problem."

Lindsay, who was hanging up a modest vintage dress she had picked up from one of Antique Row's more reputable stores, turned and looked at the doll with disgust. "*Blech.* It belongs in the trash. And we don't have a *problem.* You just have a dirty mind."

"Honey, it's been almost a *year.*"

"What did I tell you? I don't want to talk about it. I just need time."

Jeff sighed. "Yeah, you keep saying that."

Without a response, Lindsay left the room.

Later that evening, Jeff brushed his teeth, got in bed, and cracked open one of his legal thrillers. His nose was buried deep in the book when the bedroom door opened, and Lindsay walked in wearing a flimsy lace lingerie with scarlet straps, highlighting a shapely body she normally kept hidden.

"Honey?" asked Jeff. He was caught completely off guard.

135

"Hey, baby." Lindsay smiled seductively, a simper he hadn't seen in ages. She walked slowly to the bed. Jeff sniffed the air, thinking she might be drunk, but she hadn't had a lick. She got in bed and the two explored each other in uniquely unrestrained ways. As with the Framptons, the Buckinghams' room became almost unbearably warm, their ardent interactions engulfing the room with their body heat.

Fifteen minutes later, they were lying on their backs, sweaty and out of breath. Jeff exhaled deeply and smiled. He was about to fall asleep, when Lindsay suddenly straddled him. She wanted more, and she got it. Then twice more in the middle of the night. She was insatiable.

Before passing out from exhaustion around 3 a.m., Jeff looked at the fertility doll standing on his dresser and grinned. He didn't believe in magic, but it certainly hadn't been a mood killer, that was for sure.

The next several months were blissful for the Framptons and the Buckinghams. Their marriages, which had grown frustrating and lifeless, were both suddenly reinvigorated.

Marsha was physically fulfilled for the first time in years. Allen pounced on her every night, and she reciprocated his passion. Eventually, his drive became so intense, however, that she was having trouble keeping up with him, and left him many a night wanting more. She thought about the fertility doll and wondered whether if, in some way, it really was working. Allen's erectile dysfunction and sluggishness in the bedroom had soured their love life for some time, and he had suddenly, almost miraculously, been cured and acquired the stamina of a man twenty years his junior.

She picked the tiny, wooden woman off the shelf and held it in her hands. Her fingers ran along the grooves of its eyes and over its nubby chest. *Surely, nothing so small, some piece of wood, could have any real influence on her life, could it?* Dr. Marvelry had told them that it derived its power from being paired with the other doll. *Even if magic or any sort of mumbo-jumbo like that did exist, the doll shouldn't work anyway, right?* Out

136

of nowhere, she felt a sudden fire in her loins, an unexpected desire to touch herself. She looked down at the doll and a fear swept over her. Her hand was shaking as she placed the carving back on the shelf and left the room.

Unfortunately, it wasn't long before Allen began acting strange, heading out for late night walks, hiding phone conversations in other rooms. She started to suspect that he might be sleeping with other women to fulfill his extraordinary libido. Marsha had heard of sex addiction and Allen had been exhibiting the telltale signs. As quickly as their marriage had improved, it again languished due to the specter of Allen's infidelity.

Meanwhile, the Buckinghams were starting to have problems of their own. Lindsay's desire had grown so strong, much more than Jeff could handle. She uncharacteristically began returning the flirtations, and then eventually, the advances of a coworker. She didn't feel her normal, reserved self anymore, and it was exciting. Soon Lindsay was staying late at work a couple nights out of the week, and heading out to the market at all hours of the night.

Jeff suspected Lindsay was up to something. Not a month before he had called her a "cold, frigid bitch" to his buddy. Now she was practically a hedonist.

He was waiting at the kitchen table at 11:30 one night when Lindsay strolled in, a wide smile across her face.

"Have fun...shopping?" Jeff asked, his voice cutting the silence of their home.

Lindsay gasped. "Jeff! What are you doing up?"

"Oh, you know, I was just thinking how nice it would be to fuck my wife. But I suppose Bryan in marketing is already fulfilling that role for me." Before she could lie her way out of it, he took out his phone and showed her an email she had sent her coworker, complete with a photo of her bare breasts.

Lindsay started sobbing. "Jeff, honey. You don't understand. Something's come over me. It's like I'm possessed or something. Like somebody turned on a switch. I just want to get off day and night now. Nothing satisfies me

137

anymore." She revealed to her husband that Bryan was only one of the three men she had been with that week alone, and that she had already made plans to meet with a new guy the coming weekend.

Jeff went to bed alone that night; Lindsay took the sofa. When he looked across the room at the fertility doll, his face twisted into a scowl. Like Marsha, he didn't exactly believe it to be some hexed artifact, but it did remind him of his wife's betrayal. He stomped over to the dresser and picked up the carving. In the dark, the doll's grotesque features and oversized head took on a nightmarish quality, as if it had been fashioned by some malevolent artisan. He threw it at the wall, but it bounced off with a loud thud and fell to the floor, completely intact.

Within weeks of visiting Dr. Marvelry's shop, both the Buckinghams and Frampton marriages were unrecognizable.

Lindsay, her infidelity already out in the open, went on what could only be described as a sex spree. She made the rounds of every major dating site, meeting up with dozens of men, practically emasculating them with her ferocity and sexual prowess. But no matter how many men claimed to be up to the task, she couldn't find her equal in the bedroom.

She was perusing Cupid's Arrow, a site for casual encounters, when she came upon a profile for a newer member: Allen Frampton. What caught her eye were the number of negative reviews and messages he had already accumulated from his short time on the site, and that he proudly displayed on his front page: "Sex was great. He wasn't," "He's a player, ladies," and so on. A couple chat sessions later, Lindsay was in bed with the man, pushing him to his limit, and he hers. Their encounters were animalistic in their intensity and disregard for societal norms. Their "sessions" became so frequent, so cataclysmic, that they both called into work sick, morning after morning, to keep their streak alive.

138

Weeks passed and, mistaking their lust for something of substance, Allen and Lindsay revealed their relationship to their already defeated and disgusted spouses, professing their devotion to each other. Separation papers were issued not long after.

As their family life crumbled around them, Allen and Lindsay decided it best to just move in together. Each brought a fertility doll to their new apartment, as their ex-spouses couldn't stand the sight of the idols. The dolls were a pair once again, side by side, in the couple's new bedroom.

What had seemed like the most passionate, wild relationship imaginable just days and weeks previous, had as soon deteriorated into a singular monotony. Allen, who had attained the stamina of a raging bull, suddenly had performance issues, suffering what he jokingly referred to as "stage fright." Lindsay, on the other hand, grew depressed and reverted to her old self, disinterested in intercourse, thinking it a chore.

It wasn't a month before the couple called it quits, both realizing that their relationship was founded on nothing. By then, it was too late to go groveling back to their spouses. The separations had been made legal, and Marsha and Jeff didn't want to hear a word from them.

On the day they moved out of their still-new apartment, Allen and Lindsay tossed their respective fertility carvings—a symbol of love and family, not lust—into the trash and went their separate ways.

140

-Preview-

Chapter Two: The Hapless Eidolon
(from the novella *Carol for a Haunted Man*)

Jacob stood outside his cousin Ted's large colonial home nestled in the hills of Lestershire, self-conscious of his dated, shabby sweater, aware that it more acutely reflected his miserable mental state than the state of his style or finances. Ted was a successful real estate lawyer with a stunning wife named Helen and three precious children. Jacob felt like a shell of a man showing up at his cousin's impressive home holding a store-bought pumpkin pie, absent his children. But rather than face the most familial of holidays in isolation, he had accepted Ted's hospitality and would try to suffer it—if only for his mother, Rhonda, and his favorite aunt, Shirley.

The door opened, and Ted accosted Jacob with a lively, if not ingratiating, "Happy Thanksgiving, *Pilgrim!*" Barrel-chested and dapper in his fine cashmere sweater, Ted loomed over Jacob. Ted had endured many rugby games in college, and even though he had gained a few pounds brought on by long office hours and fatherhood, his lightly scarred hands and chin still struck an imposing, masculine image.

Jacob paused, managing a weak smile at Ted's shoddy, and quite dated, John Wayne impression, but ultimately wished his cousin the same.

"So, how are the kids?" asked Ted, as he led Jacob through the foyer, which was festively decorated with garland, gold bulbs, and a large decorative cornucopia set on the entranceway table. Smells of roast turkey and pumpkin spice-scented candles filled the room—a stark contrast to Jacob's new home, with its leftover Halloween-themed doormat the only recognition of the season.

"They're good," said Jacob, uncertain. In just months, his bond with his children had diminished immeasurably, and he felt unfit to elaborate on their status.

Ted led Jacob into his equally impressive living room, where the family sat watching the Macy's Day Parade. Jacob was greeted with pitying smiles from Shirley and Rhonda, who knew all too well the sad state of his nuclear family.

The next few hours were a study in envy and resentment for Jacob. He watched as Ted and his brood partook in one holiday tradition after another—backyard football, pie decorating, charades, *A Charlie Brown Thanksgiving*—the sort of traditions that he had begun with his own children in preceding years, which had now been broken.

Unable to bear another moment of the merrymaking, Jacob left the living room and wandered down the hall to Ted's study. His cousin kept a small liquor cabinet, and Jacob made short shrift of a bottle of whiskey, taking one swig after another as he admired Ted's leather furniture and collection of rare history books.

Jacob stumbled out of the study, just as Ted was making his way down the hallway in search of his absent cousin.

"What are you doing?" Ted asked. "You've been gone a while. I thought you were sick in the bathroom or something."

"Just having a drink, Ted," said Jacob, nonchalantly.

Ted took notice of Jacob's glassy eyes. "How much did you have?"

Jacob paused. "Listen. I'll buy you a new bottle, okay?"

"It's Thanksgiving, man. I know you're going through some stuff, but I don't want you drunk around my kids."

Jacob, stewing in his self-hatred like a turkey soaking in brine, allowed himself to sink further into wretchedness. His envy for Ted—composed, well-dressed, gorgeous family—seemed only to embolden him. "Oh, *fuck off*, man."

142

"*Really*, Jake?" Ted replied, searching his cousin's face for some sign of penance.

Jacob ignored him and returned to the living room, where everyone was watching football on the television. Ted followed, willing to cut his cousin some additional slack, but he was noticeably less cheery than when he had left to find Jacob.

"What did I miss?" asked Jacob. His mother quickly discerned his lush demeanor and shook her head. The children, to Ted's relief, took no notice of their cousin's condition.

"We were just about to eat dinner," said Ted, sternly. "Children, get to the table, please."

"About time," said Jacob, drawing a prolonged glare from Ted.

The family gathered in the dining room, where Helen and Shirley had set out a bounty of food. A glazed, oven-roasted turkey was set on the crisp white tablecloth, and steam rose to the high ceilings, a heavy aroma of sage and rosemary with it. Food was passed, Ted led the family in grace, and the dinner commenced.

And whether from the alcohol he had ingested, or an obscene lack of sleep, or merely his need in that moment for the comfort of an illusion, Jacob imagined an alternate path his life might have taken, where Beatrice and his children were sitting at the table with him at cousin Ted's. He thought specifically of his precious Jillian, smiling across the table, making mountains of her mashed potatoes. He was contented only briefly, before snapping out of the fantasy, and returning to the prison of his own making.

As everyone ate, Ted discussed some recent changes at his firm, his daughter Wendy's progression as a pianist, and plans for an addition to the house.

"Timmy, do you want the drumstick?" said Jacob to Ted's youngest, interrupting Ted's rich description of his future rec room. Jacob held the turkey leg aloft and motioned as if to award the boy a grand trophy. As he reached across the table, succulent flesh fell from the bone and plopped down into the gravy bowl, splashing Helen and his aunt with the greasy, brown juice.

"Noooo! This is *chiffon*," exclaimed Helen as she jumped up from the table and began vigorously scrubbing at the blotch on her dress with her napkin.

Jacob put the bone down and looked around the table. All his extended family (except for young Timmy), even his own mother, glowered at him and the mess he had made of their meal.

"*Relax*, it'll come out," said Jacob, snickering to himself over Helen's overreaction.

"Is something *funny*, Jake?!" said Ted, raising his voice.

"I'll buy you a new goddamn dress...and tablecloth. Christ."

Ted sprung from his chair and stared down his cousin. "Watch your mouth! My kids don't need to hear your filth."

"Jacob, seriously?" chimed in Rhonda.

Jacob rolled his eyes. "Calm down, Ted. They'll live," he said, before belching.

"Hey! You may not give a damn about how your kids are raised, but when you're in *my* house, you'll act like an adult and set a good example."

Jacob fumed, gripping his fork tightly. "You don't know the first thing about my kids."

"I know enough," said Ted, smirking at his sad, cuckolded cousin.

"Jacob, cut the crap," said Rhonda.

"Ugh, this is *never* going to come out!" whined Helen, continuing her vain attempt to remove the stain, unaware of the escalating situation.

Jacob stood, and in one swift motion, he grabbed the tablecloth and yanked it toward him, causing the entirety of the table's contents to tumble over into a mess of mashed potatoes, yams, and cranberry sauce. The adults jumped back and the children screamed as plates fell onto the plush, white carpet, and champagne glasses shattered against the table.

No one spoke—even Ted was too shocked to respond—while Jacob excused himself, grabbed his coat from the foyer, and began the long walk home.

A chill, sobering breeze seemed to follow Jacob as he made the mile-long trek through Lestershire's north side. He caught himself lingering in front of a few of the homes with packed driveways and cars overflowing into the street—the hallmarks of celebratory gatherings. Thinking of the families and friends at dinner tables inside, laughing, chatting, reminiscing, and enjoying each other's company. He considered his own children and the fun they were likely having, playing with his wife's nieces and nephews, and eating their favorite pies and desserts. They were a handful, especially with the added stress of holiday obligations, but their difficulty was nothing when compared to the heartache of spending Thanksgiving alone.

Rather than face the rest of the holiday in his empty home, Jacob took a slight detour down to the Oasis, a small pub which he now frequented, more so since the divorce had been finalized. The bar had been there since he was a boy, and it provided him some comfort to walk through the door and recall the trips he had taken with (and sometimes to retrieve) his father over the years.

The Oasis was a Lestershire institution, occupying the same nondescript building for nearly eight decades. In the mid-20th century it had been a popular watering hole for workers getting off their shifts at the nearby boot factory. Even after a mass exodus of manufacturing jobs in the 1980s, which crippled Lestershire's economy, the Oasis still managed to get by. It had been renovated in recent years but still boasted its original mahogany bar top, vintage signage, and neon lights advertising beer companies that no longer existed.

Jacob was pleased to see Anna, his favorite waitress, waiting on a table as he entered. When he climbed the stairs to the dining area, Anna took notice of him and they shared a smile.

"Happy Thanksgiving, Jake! I'll be over in a minute," said Anna.

Jacob nodded and took a seat in one of the bright red vinyl booths. He watched Anna admiringly as she took the other table's order. Her cheeriness and arresting blue eyes were a welcome sight. On her feet for ten consecutive hours, she still possessed an energy that defied the bar's typically sleepy atmosphere. Jacob would often watch her manage the busy weekend crowd, admiring her striking black hair and trim figure. Lestershire's color and spirit had dimmed over the years, and even something so simple as a warm look from a pretty girl was enough to get his heart pumping.

"No plans for Thanksgiving?" asked Anna, as she approached Jacob's table.

"Dinner was over before it began, unfortunately..."

"Oh, that bad, huh?" remarked Anna, frowning. "How are the kids?"

"I don't know."

"You didn't get to see them, then?"

"Any turkey left?" said Jacob, changing the subject.

"Unfortunately, we're all out of turkey and stuffing. How about a Saranac hard cider and a hot pie?" she said, grinning.

Jacob nodded, and Anna went to the kitchen. He sat in the silence of an almost empty bar on Thanksgiving Day, watching a football game which was all but over, his mind someplace else entirely.

Anna couldn't help but notice Jacob's especially sullen demeanor when she returned with his drink.

"Jake, what's wrong?"

"You know..." he replied and sipped his drink.

She sat down across from him. He eyed her, almost suspicious of her intent. He and Anna had been cordial up to that point, but they had never discussed anything beyond the basics. He knew her uneventful life story: thirty and single, never married, no kids—and she knew he was newly divorced, had three kids, and was having a tough time adjusting to his new life.

146

"I've got time if you want to chat; it's pretty dead in here and I'm due for a break," said Anna, motioning around the bar.

Jacob nodded. It may have been the alcohol talking, but he laid his life bare before her. There was the divorce and his wife's infidelity, how he felt strangely uncomfortable in his new home, the earlier incident at his cousin's table, his inability to write anything of substance, and the problem closest to his heart—how he felt he would never get the chance to be a proper father to his children.

"They're so young, Anna. I barely know them as people. I just about begged her to give me a few more years with them, that I didn't care what she did outside the house and we could make it work for her. I want a chance to get to know them as these developing little human beings before they're all grown."

She listened closely, sympathetic to his troubles. "It really isn't fair, Jake. She's making these selfish choices despite the other four people she's hurting."

He downed the last few sips of his drink and continued: "Beatrice has always run from any type of responsibility. Ever since we were kids she couldn't handle someone relying on her for anything. It's like she has no interest in thinking about the future or learning from the past..."

Anna put her hand over Jacob's as he continued mumbling to himself. "I get it. You did what was best for your family and she did what was best for her. You deserve better."

They locked eyes briefly, each understanding something intimate about the other, if only for that moment. While Jacob had been pouring his heart and troubles out upon the table before them, he had also been inhaling Anna's heady perfume, and felt himself being drawn in by her subtle sensuality.

"I'm drunk, aren't I?" stated Jacob.

Anna nodded.

"I should go home."

147

She went into the kitchen and put his food in a box.

"You gonna make it?" asked Anna when she returned.

He chuckled. "It's just around the block. If I collapse in a bush on the way, I'm sure Mrs. Ellsic will be on the phone with the police to make the report before I die of exposure."

Anna saw Jacob to the door. "I'll walk you home if you want. It's getting pretty dark already."

He grinned, considering her offer. "Maybe some other time."

She hugged him goodbye and he headed out into the frigid, late-November air. Jacob nearly toppled over on the bottom step as he met level ground. The pizza box flipped out of his hand and fell squarely, cheese down.

"Shit!" He was drunker than he had thought, and took his time crossing the street and navigating the back alley between apartment complexes which led out onto Albany Street.

Perhaps it was the drink, but Jacob could almost *feel* the looming twilight as he made his way to Fifty Albany. He was always nervous going alone at night; the neighborhood had become slightly more menacing over the years, a tad grittier and rundown. He was acutely aware of the shadows cast by nearby houses and telephone poles, and his boyhood stomping grounds became almost unfamiliar. The driveways in his neighborhood were oddly vacant, very few of the homes lit up by family gatherings. He felt utterly isolated out in the cold, blue evening.

Jacob climbed the steep stairs that led to his front door, pausing midway to brace himself. He stared long and hard down the street at the rows of factory-built homes, searching for a would-be stalker. Spotting no one, he finished his ascent and unlocked the door. However, he found no respite upon entering his house. It was as empty and silent as ever. The air inside was thick, cool, and felt as if the structure itself was anticipating the loneliness of his return. He removed his outer layers, kicked off his shoes, and went right to the bathroom,

148

without bothering with any of the lights. As he relieved himself his eyes began to fill with tears.

His anxiety would only build as the night advanced. Jacob's dread was that of someone who knew with certainty what the future held. Days followed by nights of a father without children to guide, to impress upon. There is a moment in every father's life where he recognizes himself within his child, and in turn, recognizes his child within himself. The locus of Jacob's angst was in his living a life separated from himself, or from his other selves.

He shuffled into his bedroom and undressed slowly. He felt hunger pangs in the pit of his empty stomach as he thought of the ruined pizza he had left in the parking lot of the neighborhood bar. The day had been a wash, a fitting preview of the holiday season to come, something he anticipated he would have to survive. It wasn't even 7 p.m. when his rummy head hit the pillow, and he soon fell into a deep, yet uneasy, sleep.

He dreamt that night of walking the street outside, though from the point of view of his childhood self. It was still vaguely comforting for him to take that same sidewalk; there were still so many small details to rediscover about the physical space he had once occupied. But Dream Jacob was startled from his remembrance of things past at the sight of a skinned deer hanging in the Halicki's backyard at 36 Albany. He nearly wretched at the grisly scene. The carcass was cast from a tree by rope, its fluids still draining onto the cool grass.

Hunting was common and so were cadaverous deer, but there was something indecent at how exposed this particular creature was. Jacob continued, quickly, up the hill, pausing a moment before his parents' home, just a few houses away from his present-day address. He wondered at his own lucidity as he beheld his old front porch, the awning with its four green stripes, and his bedroom window above, which still sported the fire safety sticker.

149

Even in dream Jacob couldn't quite revisit the past in the way that he wanted. He would have enjoyed a sleep-walk through the house, to see how much of it he could put back into place before waking. But he was guided by that invisible hand within the recesses of his mind, and he kept walking.

Jacob's involuntary journey continued. He passed more familiar homes, skewed in color and construction from their real-life counterparts, until he came upon his driveway—or was it Mr. Herrick's? The house had an unquestionable presence about it, as if all the other homes on the block were shades of gray and this one was a radiant red. His attention was drawn to the neglected garage that sat at the end of its long driveway. He had never paid the garage much attention—he always parked his car in the driveway and only used the aging structure to house forgotten or broken household items, furniture in need of repair, and spare tools—but the image before him was impossible not to take note of.

He marched up the driveway, diligently, with an ill-defined sense of purpose. It had been nearly twenty years since he had last seen Mr. Herrick, but he gradually came to recognize the man's face when he saw the body hanging from a rope inside the garage. Herrick's grey, bushy moustache, pronounced chin and husky upper body were impossible not to recognize, even though the body was slack, blue and twitching. A wooden chair lay on its side on the cement floor below.

Jacob awoke in a bed-sodden sweat. He knew Thomas Herrick hadn't hanged himself. The man had passed in the local hospital's intensive care unit from pneumonia—at least that is what his father had told him. It was still before daybreak, but he decided to get out of bed, run laundry, and clean the house, since his children would be over that day.

It wasn't long before Beatrice, who wished to while the day away shopping for discount gifts, left the children with him. As was tradition, he took them to breakfast at his favorite downtown diner, then to the Christmas tree farm he had been going to since he was a boy. He was excited to carry on this tradition, despite the fact that the tree wouldn't stand in his own home, but Beatrice's.

Everett, Jordan, and Jillian trailed their father up the hill, amidst row after row of coniferous trees, Jacob carrying with him a small, rusty handsaw. The country air was brisk and thick with the familiar smell of pine needles, and he inhaled with a joy that surprised him. The landscape was short of picturesque; there was no snow to speak of, just a field of brown grass, split by dirt tracks and an uncountable assortment of green trees.

"Daddy, this one!" said his daughter, Jillian, pointing at a wide Douglas fir with dark-green needles in one of the first rows they came to. She rushed toward the tree and her younger brothers followed, kicking up a cloud of dirt in their wake. The twins' interest was solely in the exploratory nature of the trip, as they showed no reverence for their father's search for the symbol itself.

"Sweetheart, we can look around some more. There might be an even better one up farther!" said Jacob, wanting to prolong their experience.

"No, Daddy, this one's fantastic," replied Jillian, as she yanked at the tiny needles like petals from a flower.

"Okay. No problem." Jacob shrugged his shoulders, bent down, and began to saw at the hearty trunk, which was as thick as his bicep. He paused to make sure his trouble-prone four-year-olds were within eyesight. "Everett, Jordan, don't you dare wander off!"

Spotting them kicking rocks not far away, he went back to work on the tree trunk. When he was midway through, he looked up again to check on his two youngest, as they were oddly quiet.

"Where the heck are your brothers?!" yelled Jacob. "*Goddammit*!!" He had lost his concentration mid-pull and cut a deep gash in the webbing of his bracing hand, between the thumb and forefinger.

151

"Is that blood, Daddy?" asked Jillian.

Jacob gawked at his gushing hand, then locked eyes with his unshaken daughter before his vision faded to black.

"Where are my kids?" Jacob asked, lightheaded after regaining consciousness in an ambulance.

"They're being taken care of, sir. They're with the Cole's, the family that runs the tree farm," replied the attending medic.

"All three of them?"

"Yes, sir. That little girl of yours is a bright one. She knew your wife's cell number and they were able to get ahold of her. They're good people—your kids will be fine."

"My ex-wife." Jacob momentarily forgot his physical trauma, feeling a pang of a different sort at the thought of Beatrice's involvement.

"Okay, sir. You lost a decent amount of blood back there and we're taking you to the ER. Hopefully it'll just be a few stitches."

The ambulance pulled into the emergency room entrance. Jacob rode the stretcher into a room that resembled something more akin to a utility closet and was left alone without explanation. Over the next few hours he was visited by various hospital personnel and left numerous messages on Beatrice's voicemail asking, and then begging, her to call him. Finally, a doctor arrived to stitch and wrap his hand.

As Jacob waited to be released, Beatrice finally returned his call. "How's your hand?" she asked, flatly.

"Eight stitches. Doesn't really hurt, but they have me on pain meds. Are the kids okay?"

"Are the kids *okay*?" Beatrice's tone quickly turned venomous. "Jacob, you abandoned your kids at a tree farm. What were you thinking? That woman, Mrs. Cole, told me they found Jordan wandering the field by himself."

She caught her breath and continued before Jacob could interject. "You're a lousy father and have never paid enough attention to your kids. You really need to take some time and

152

think about how you can actually be present when you're with them. Goodbye!"

Beatrice hung up after her tirade and Jacob didn't bother trying to call her back. He knew she had her mind set on withholding the kids, and he considered whether she might be right in doing so. He called a cab and was back at his house by early evening, leaving him hours before sleep to wallow over his tarnished tradition.

Jacob's hand began to throb as he heated up some canned tomato soup, so he downed a few of the prescribed pain pills. His loss that day was of more than just the use of his left hand, or even the botching of a memorable experience for him and his children. No, the major casualty of that Black Friday was his hope for the future and the holiday season itself. Christmas and New Year's no longer held any promise or the possibility of a rekindling of spirit.

Jacob sat with his bowl of soup in his chair beside the chimney, worn out by the day and the medication. He refrained from playing any holiday television or music; he had but the quiet of a desolate heart for company, beating its meaningless beats into a vast nothingness. He thought groggily of the small traditions he and his sisters kept decades before, just a few houses away. If time travel or astral projection were possible by way of thought alone, he would have discovered its secrets that night. He immersed himself in the memory of being part of a family that celebrated Thanksgivings and Christmases with countless common and a few unique ways of doing things. The preparation for the experience of a day, or an evening, was as important as the celebration itself.

The way in which the stockings or ornaments were hung, when and where was it acceptable to display such things, what the items uniquely represented to different members of the family—the details of the customs brought him comfort in remembrance. He thought of what happened to these shared beliefs once his family had grown and split apart, how the ideas had transposed and transformed in the different households, how he no longer had a fighting chance at passing on his own variation of the things that once brought him comfort and joy.

Had Jacob been sober-minded at the time, he would have written down a portion of his racing thoughts for some future work of fiction. Maybe he would have channeled his wealth of emotion into characters and plot and put this wellspring to good use. But instead, he gradually turned from the warmth of sentimentality to the bleak depths of the despair of his present, and what he could prognosticate of his future.

He let the soup cool on the small lamp table beside him and sunk into his chair, content to retreat into the misery of remembrance, knowing that the best moments of the past could never truly be replayed. That a blessed childhood seemed to span ages, and each adult decade was of a different character entirely. Adult years quickly become short and fleeting, with only rare moments of minor contentment.

His thoughts returned him to the house he inhabited. Had he not been so cerebral and explorative in that moment, he might have missed the slight shadow on the far wall. It was his struggle with his experience of past joys against his own present heartache and the despair which seemingly fueled the materialization of the figure. Jacob focused on the shape and, like a waking dream, the shape came to be. Not a ghoul nor an outline of a some-thing, but a three-dimensional being that one would give no second thought to, or have issue with, passing on the street.

A man in full had appeared before Jacob in his living room.

Acknowledgments

Like the characters within these pages, it is our relationships which truly define us, and we'd be remiss not to mention those who've been our inspiration and support in creating this book, especially Burt, for yet another thoughtful read-through; Ben, for a stunning cover design; our partners, Sybil and Emily, for encouraging our hobby; and Zinger, for his eternal love and devotion.

Made in the USA
Las Vegas, NV
23 April 2023

70980408R00094